The Big Book of

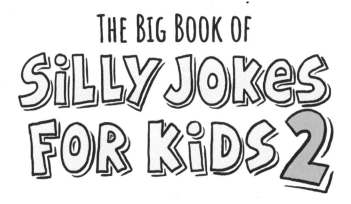

SiLLY JOKeS
FOR KiDS 2

The Big Book of Silly Jokes for Kids 2

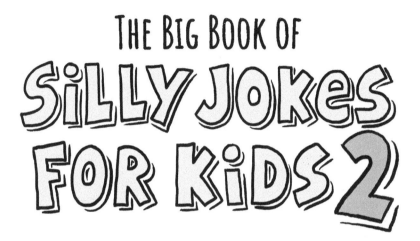

Carole P. Roman

Illustrations by

Dylan Goldberger

ROCKRIDGE
PRESS

Copyright © 2020 by Rockridge Press, Emeryville, California

No part of this publication may be reproduced, stored in a retrieval system, or transmitted in any form or by any means, electronic, mechanical, photocopying, recording, scanning, or otherwise, except as permitted under Sections 107 or 108 of the 1976 United States Copyright Act, without the prior written permission of the Publisher. Requests to the Publisher for permission should be addressed to the Permissions Department, Rockridge Press, 6005 Shellmound Street, Suite 175, Emeryville, CA 94608.

Limit of Liability/Disclaimer of Warranty: The Publisher and the author make no representations or warranties with respect to the accuracy or completeness of the contents of this work and specifically disclaim all warranties, including without limitation warranties of fitness for a particular purpose. No warranty may be created or extended by sales or promotional materials. The advice and strategies contained herein may not be suitable for every situation. This work is sold with the understanding that the Publisher is not engaged in rendering medical, legal, or other professional advice or services. If professional assistance is required, the services of a competent professional person should be sought. Neither the Publisher nor the author shall be liable for damages arising herefrom. The fact that an individual, organization, or website is referred to in this work as a citation and/or potential source of further information does not mean that the author or the Publisher endorses the information the individual, organization, or website may provide or recommendations they/it may make. Further, readers should be aware that websites listed in this work may have changed or disappeared between when this work was written and when it is read.

For general information on our other products and services or to obtain technical support, please contact our Customer Care Department within the United States at (866) 744-2665, or outside the United States at (510) 253-0500.

Rockridge Press publishes its books in a variety of electronic and print formats. Some content that appears in print may not be available in electronic books, and vice versa.

TRADEMARKS: Rockridge Press and the Rockridge Press logo are trademarks or registered trademarks of Callisto Media Inc. and/or its affiliates, in the United States and other countries, and may not be used without written permission. All other trademarks are the property of their respective owners. Rockridge Press is not associated with any product or vendor mentioned in this book.

Interior and Cover Designer: Eric Pratt
Art Producer: Hannah Dickerson
Editor: Erin Nelson
Production Manager: Riley Hoffman
Production Editor: Melissa Edeburn

Illustrations © Dylan Goldberger, 2020 | dylangoldberger.com

ISBN: Print 978-1-64739-603-9 | eBook 978-1-64739-378-6

R0

For my kids and grandkids,
who never fail to amuse me.
Special thanks to Erin
and Joe, without whom
this book would not have
been written.

If you're too busy to

LAUGH,

you are too busy.

— Proverb

Contents

BUCKLE UP...

...and get ready for a barrel of laughs! Just when you thought you couldn't giggle any more, *The Big Book of Silly Jokes for Kids 2* is here with more fun ways to tickle your family and friends.

Perfect for practicing your joke-telling skills, this book is jam-packed with hundreds of riddles, knock-knock jokes, funny stories, and more to help you develop your punny bone. Did I say *punny*? There are puns in here, too! Don't forget to check out the last chapter and learn to write some new jokes of your own. Creating and telling jokes is a great way to introduce yourself to new friends, stretch your brain, and get lost in the silliness of being a kid.

So, cheer up your best friend, make Mom or Dad laugh, surprise Grandpa with a funny story of your own, and—most important—bring people together in the best way possible. Humor is the fastest way to friendship, fun-filled memories, and glee!

Silly Q & A

What do you get when you cross a rabbit with a snake?
A jump rope.

What event do spiders love to attend?
Webbings.

What do snowmen call their kids?
Chill-dren.

Why didn't the girl trust the ocean?
There was something fishy about it.

Why are skeletons happy?
Because nothing gets under their skin.

How do you make an egg roll?
You push it.

What's a boxer's favorite drink?
Punch.

Why was the man running around his bed?
He wanted to catch up on his sleep.

Where do you find Mexico?
On the map.

Why do witches ride on broomsticks?
Because it's faster than walking.

What does Dracula drive?
A monster truck.

What do you call a fish's date?
His gill-friend.

What's a frog's favorite year?
A leap year.

Silly Stat: A leap year comes once every four years. Julius Caesar, a ruler of the Roman Empire, is considered the "father" of leap year because of the calendar he created based on an ancient Egyptian one. Leap day babies, born on February 29, are called "leapers" or "leaplings." A baby being born today has a 1 in 1,461 chance of being a leapling.

What do ants eat
for breakfast?
Croiss-ants.

What do aliens call a
zany spaceperson?
An astro-*nut*.

What type of bat
loves doorbells?
A *ding*-bat.

How did the Vikings
send secret messages?
Norse code.

Silly Stat: The words
"Norse" and "Viking"
describe the Germanic
people who settled
in Scandinavia during
the Viking Age. They
spoke a language
called "Old Norse."
The "Norse" refers to
Norsemen (sounds
like "horsemen!"), who
were full-time traders.

What kind of band
can't play music?
A rubber band.

What do you hold without
using your hands?
Your breath.

What did the bologna
say to the salami?
"Nice to meat you."

What is a snake's favorite
subject in school?
Hissssstory.

What kind of bed does
a mermaid sleep in?
A waterbed.

What should you
never say to a vampire
when you are mad?
"Bite me!"

Why was school easier
for cavemen?
Because they had no
history to study.

What does a cat say when
you step on its tail?
"Mee-ouch!"

What time is it when ten gorillas are chasing you?
Ten after one.

What are a plumber's favorite shoes?
Clogs.

What do ghosts say when they meet?
"How do you boo?"

Why did the computer get glasses?
To improve its website.

What dog always knows what time it is?
A watchdog.

What is a ghost's favorite tree?
Bamboo.

What do you call a boo-boo on a T. rex?
A dino-sore.

Which side of a cat has the most fur?
The outside.

Did you hear about the dog that ate a clock?
He got ticks.

What does a frog do when his car breaks down?
He gets toad away.

Why do we say "break a leg" to actors?
Because they want to be in a cast.

Silly Stat: The English expression "break a leg" is what people say to actors to wish them good luck before a performance. It is always taken as words of encouragement and has been used since Shakespeare's days. Outside of theater, it's a way to say, "Good luck! Put your best foot forward."

What day of the week are most twins born?
Twos-days.

Why did the broom get
a bad grade in class?
Because it was always
sweeping during class.

How do you stop a bull
from charging?
You unplug it.

Why do mummies
like presents?
They love the wrapping.

What's the longest
word in the world?
"Smiles." There is a
mile between its first
and last letters.

What do you get when
you cross a sponge
and an electric eel?
A shock absorber.

Why did the banana go
out with the blueberry?
Because she couldn't
find a date.

What kind of soda
does a tree like?
Root beer.

What do you call a turkey
after Thanksgiving?
Lucky.

Why did the scarecrow
quit his job?
Everything he did
was for the birds.

What do you call a bear
that loves rainy weather?
A drizzly bear.

What's a matador's
favorite sandwich?
Bull-oney.

Silly Stat: Up until recently, bullfighting was a major sport in Spain. "Matador" is the name for the bullfighter, who wears a special hat as part of their costume. The two round bulbs on either side of the hat represent the bull's horns. The flattened crown of the hat is meant to look like a bull's eye.

What do you call a
walking clock?
Time travel.

What do basketball players
and babies have in common?
They're expert dribblers.

What do you get when you
cross a rabbit and a cow?
A hare in your milk.

What kind of paper
likes hip-hop?
Rapping paper.

What's a vampire's
favorite fruit?
A neck-tarine.

Why did the
computer squeak?
Someone stepped
on its mouse.

What do you call
a mean cow?
Beef jerky.

What kind of lights did
Noah use on the ark?
Floodlights.

What's the best way
to carve wood?
Whittle by whittle.

Silly Stat: Whittling is the art of carving small figures out of pieces of wood. Creating tiny works of art became a popular pastime for men, even General Ulysses S. Grant, to fill their time during the Civil War.

What time is it when you
see half a dozen chickens?
Six o'cluck.

What's the Joker's
favorite candy?
Snickers.

What's the noisiest sport?
Tennis—it's a racket!

What did the sun say
when it was introduced
to the earth?
"Pleased to heat you."

What do you call an eagle who plays the piano?
Talon-ted.

Silly Stat: A talon is the nail or claw of an animal and is made of a hard protein called keratin. Its many uses include digging, climbing, fighting, capturing, and holding prey. Talons are largest and most prominent on carnivorous birds, such as hawks, eagles, and owls, that need to catch and eat their prey.

What do you get when you cross a cat and a lemon?
A sourpuss.

Who makes clothes for a stegosaurus?
A dino-sewer.

What kind of horses only go out at night?
Nightmares.

Who did the mummy invite to his party?
Anybody he could dig up.

How do blue jays stay fit?
Worm-ups.

Why was the tarantula wearing a mask?
Because it was a spy-der.

What wobbles and flies?
A jelly-copter.

Why did the hamburger always lose the race?
Because it could never ketchup.

Why didn't the student get in trouble when he was caught passing notes?
Because it was music class.

What do you get when you mix history with old oil?
Ancient grease.

What sound does a metal frog make?
Rivet, rivet.

Silly Stat: Rosie the Riveter was a popular cultural icon during World War II. You might have seen her on the poster that shows her flexed arm! Her character inspired women to take jobs in factories and shipyards while men were at war. Since then, Rosie has become a symbol of equality and expanding opportunities for women in industries dominated by men.

What table doesn't have any legs?
A multiplication table.

What is always cold in the refrigerator?
Chili.

What's a teacher's favorite nation?
Explanation.

What do you call a fossil who won't go to work?
Lazy bones.

What does a vampire say to a mirror?
"Is this thing on?"

Why did the pig become an actor?
Because he was a ham.

> **Silly Stat:** The word "ham" is used to refer to an actor who gives an exaggerated performance.

Why did the cucumber call 911?
Because he was in a pickle.

How do movie stars stay cool?
They sit next to their fans.

What do you get when you cross a bee with some meat?
A hum-burger.

Where does a television go for vacation?
Remote islands.

What did Delaware wear to the soccer game?
A New Jersey.

What do you always get for your birthday?
Older.

Why was the guy looking for fast food on his friend?
Because his friend said, "Dinner is on me."

What is a witch's favorite day of the week?
Fright-day.

Why are cats good at playing video games?
Because they have nine lives.

> **Silly Stat:** For years, a myth developed that cats had multiple lives. In parts of Spain, it is believed that cats have seven lives, whereas Turkish and Arabic legends say cats have six lives. No one knows exactly where the expression came from, but it has been around for many years! Even William Shakespeare used the expression in his famous play *Romeo and Juliet*.

Why did Keisha put on her helmet when working on her computer?
She thought it would crash.

What do you get when you cross a refrigerator with a radio?
Cool music.

Pronounce the word M-O-S-T.
"Most."
Pronounce the word G-H-O-S-T.
"Ghost."
Pronounce the word B-O-A-S-T.
"Boast."
What do you put in the toaster?
"Toast?"
No! You put bread in the toaster and get toast out.

What asks but never answers?
An owl. ("Whooo whoooo!")

What did the werewolf eat after he got his teeth cleaned?
His dentist.

What do you call a dentist who cleans a lion's teeth?
Adventurous.

What's a pirate's favorite kind of fish?
Goldfish.

How do you cut a wave in half?
With a sea-saw.

What has 13 hearts but no organs?
A deck of cards.

Why didn't the invisible man buy a house?
He couldn't see himself living there.

What do you get when you put an iPhone in the blender?
Apple juice.

What are two things you never eat for lunch?
Breakfast and dinner.

What happens when an owl gets a sore throat?
It doesn't give a hoot.

How many sides does a circle have?
Two: an inside and an outside.

Who is the highest-ranking officer in a cornfield?
The kernel.

What did the dalmatian say after lunch?
"That hit the spot."

Silly Stat: Dalmatians are often associated with firehouses. In the olden days, fire trucks or carriages were pulled by horses, but the horses would get nervous around fires. The dalmatians were used because of their ability to keep the horses calm.

Why are mummies so selfish?
Because they are all wrapped up in themselves.

Why did the chicken cross the ocean?
To get to the other tide.

What did one snowman say to the other snowman?
Do you smell carrots?

Why should you put a spiderweb on your baseball glove?
To catch flies.

How do you find an archery contest?
Follow the arrows.

What do postal workers do when they get mad?
They stamp their feet.

Silly Stat: On July 1, 1847, in New York City, postage stamps first went on sale. Benjamin Franklin's face was on the five-cent stamp. George Washington was on the 10-cent stamp. It's fitting that Ben Franklin was honored, since he was the first postmaster general in the United States!

What do you call a bear without ears?
B.

What's a vampire's favorite superhero?
Batman.

What kind of nails do carpenters hate hammering?
Fingernails.

What do you call bees having a bad hair day?
Frizz-bees.

Silly Stat: Honeybees are great fliers. They fly at speeds around 15 miles per hour and beat their wings 200 times per second!

What do you call a bear with no socks on?
Bear-foot.

Why is the Hulk a good gardener?
Because he has a green thumb.

Why did the rooster cross the road?
To prove he wasn't a chicken.

What's the scariest ride at the amusement park?
The roller ghoster.

Silly Stat: The Formula Rossa in Abu Dhabi, located in the United Arab Emirates, is the fastest roller coaster in the world. It clocks in at a speed of 149.1 miles per hour! Hold on to your hat.

Why do tigers have stripes?
So they aren't spotted.

What do you call a penguin in Florida?
Lost.

How do you make a hot dog stand?
Take away its chair.

What's a woodpecker's favorite joke?
Knock, knock!

What's a duck's favorite snack?
Cheese and quackers.

Why did the witch put her broom in the washer?
She wanted a clean sweep.

Why did the octopus beat the shark in a fight?
He was well-armed.

Are monsters good at math?
Not unless you Count Dracula.

Can a kangaroo jump higher than the Statue of Liberty?
Of course! The Statue of Liberty can't jump at all.

How do you weigh a fish?
Use their scales!

Why is everyone so tired on April 1?
Because they just finished a long, 31-day March.

What do you call a flower that runs on electricity?
A power plant.

How do you stop a skunk from smelling?
Hold its nose.

Silly Stat: A skunk's stripe points its way directly to the place where the smelly spray comes out! Skunks can shoot their sulfur-smelling odor up to 10 feet from their backsides. That smell can sometimes last for weeks and can be smelled as far away as a mile.

Why didn't the flower ride its bike to school?
Because the petals were broken.

What did the elephant say when it walked into the post office?
"Ouch."

Why couldn't the pirate go to the movie?
It was rated "arrrr."

How do skeletons call each other?
With tele-bones.

Silly Stat: The human skeleton is made up of about 300 bones at birth. As we age, bones fuse together, bringing the total to 206 bones.

What kind of street does a ghost live on?
A dead end.

What kind of driver has no arms or legs?
A screwdriver.

What type of dogs do vampires like?
Bloodhounds.

Who delivers presents to dogs?
Santa Paws.

Why do gorillas have big nostrils?
Because they have big fingers!

**What's the craziest
way to travel?**
Loco-motive.

Silly Stat: A locomotive
is an engine that pulls
a train supplying its
power. Early locomotives
used horses or ropes.
Today, the fastest train
in the world is the THSR
700T. It runs on a high-
speed line between
Kaohsiung and Taipei
in Taiwan. It travels at
190 miles per hour! It
shortens a trip of 4 hours
to only 90 minutes.

**What only works after
it's been fired?**
A rocket.

**What did the dog say when
he sat on sandpaper?**
"Ruff."

**What do you call a
rabbit with fleas?**
Bugs Bunny.

**What animal has more
lives than a cat?**

A frog. It croaks every night.

Why don't ghosts like rain?
It dampens their spirits.

**What do you put in a
barrel to make it lighter?**
A hole.

**Where do you find
flying rabbits?**
In the hare force.

**What did the porcupine
say to the cactus?**
"Is that you, Mom?"

**Why did the baseball coach
go into the kitchen?**
To get a pitcher.

**How much do dead
batteries charge?**
Nothing. They're
free of charge.

Why should you be nice to the dentist?
You'll hurt his fillings.

Silly Stat: Human adults usually have 32 teeth: eight incisors, four front teeth on the upper and lower jaws, four canines, eight premolars, and lastly four wisdom teeth. "Wisdom teeth" got their name because they are the last to grow, when a person is older and wiser.

What do you call an owl that does magic tricks?
Hoo-dini.

How do librarians catch fish?
With bookworms.

What do you call a belt with a watch on it?
A waist of time.

Why did the boy take a ruler to bed?
To see how long he slept.

Why was the orange so lonely?
Because the banana split.

Why was the droid angry?
Everyone kept pushing its buttons.

What are the artist's favorite shoes?
Sketchers.

How much money does a skunk have?
Too many scents.

What country do sharks come from?
Finland.

What did Neptune say to Saturn?
"Give me a ring sometime."

How do fungi clean their house?
With a mush-broom.

What do you call a sheep
covered in chocolate?
A candy baaaaaa.

Silly Stat: The first chocolate bar was made by Joseph Fry in England in 1847. He pressed a paste made from cocoa powder and sugar into the rectangle shape. Today, Americans eat 2.8 billion pounds, or about 11 pounds per person, of chocolate each year!

What's the quietest sport?
Bowling. You can
hear a pin drop.

What did the astronaut
say to the star?
"Stop spacing out."

How do you say farewell to
a three-headed monster?
"Bye, bye, bye."

What happened when
the cat swallowed
a ball of wool?
She had mittens.

What do you call it when a
cat wins at the dog show?
A cat-has-trophy.

What do you call a deer
that costs a dollar?
A buck.

What did one penny say
to the other penny?
We make perfect cents.

How do chickens encourage
their baseball team?
They egg them on.

How much room should
you give fungi to grow?
As mushroom as possible.

What time is it when a
bear sits on your bed?
Time to get a new bed!

What medicine do you
give a dog with a fever?
Mustard is the best
thing for a hot dog.

Which side of the house do pine trees grow?
The outside.

What's a balloon's least favorite school activity?
A pop quiz.

Silly Stat: In 2017, the United States produced over 8 billion coins to circulate in the country! Pennies, nickels, dimes, quarters, half-dollars, and dollar coins are all produced in the Philadelphia and Denver mints. These mints aren't for your breath! A mint is an industrial facility that prints money.

How did Ben Franklin feel after he discovered electricity?
Shocked.

What happened when the mouse fell into the bathtub?
He came out squeaky-clean.

What's better than finding a heads-up penny?
Finding a heads-up quarter.

What's the strongest tool in the ocean?
A hammerhead shark.

Why did the little girl take a hammer to her birthday cake?
It was a pound cake.

How do hedgehogs kiss?
Very carefully.

What would a vampire never order in a restaurant?
A stake sandwich.

Silly Stat: According to vampire folklore, one of the ways to stop a vampire is to push a strong wooden or metal post called a stake through their heart.

Why don't snails fart?
Their houses don't have any windows.

Why did the doughnut visit the dentist?
It got a new filling.

How do you make an egg giggle?
You tell it a funny yolk.

What do you get when you cross a shark and a cow?
I don't know, but I wouldn't try milking it.

What do you call a messy hippo?
A hippopota-mess.

Why are giraffes slow to apologize?
It takes them a long time to swallow their pride.

What did the sink say to the dirty dishes?
"You're in hot water now."

What do you get when you cross a bunch of monkeys with an orchestra?
A chimp-phony.

What kind of hair does the ocean have?
Wavy.

What did one blade of grass say to the other during a drought?
"I guess we'll have to make dew."

Where can you find an ocean with no water?
On a map.

What does a piece of toast wear to bed?
Jammies.

Why is a sofa like a Thanksgiving turkey?
They're both filled with stuffing.

What has a bed that you can't sleep in?
A river.

Where does "Friday" come before "Monday"?
In the dictionary.

What is it called when a snowman has a temper tantrum?
A meltdown!

What did the fisherman say to the magician?
Pick a cod, any cod.

What do you call a thieving alligator?
A crook-o-dile.

Why did the cow cross the road?
To get to the udder side.

What kind of fish can perform surgery?
Sturgeons.

Silly stat: "Sturgeon" is the name for 27 species of fish that belong to the Acipenseridae family. Their evolution dates back to the Triassic period—more than 200 million years ago!

What's an astronaut's favorite part of a computer?
The space bar.

What did the red light say to the green light?
"Don't look, I'm changing."

Why did the pig get hired by the restaurant?
He was really good at bacon.

What do you call a sad puppy that likes fruit?
Melon collie.

Why do French people like to eat snails?
They can't stand fast food.

What do you get when you cross a cocker spaniel, a poodle, and a rooster?
A cocker-poodle-doo!

Why does yogurt love going to museums?
Because it's cultured.

What do you throw out when you need it and take in when you don't?
An anchor.

Why was the cat sitting on the computer?
To keep an eye on the mouse!

What's a pirate's favorite treat?
Chips ahoy, matey!

What did the baby corn ask the mommy corn?
"Where's Pop corn?"

What's a cat's favorite television show?
The evening mews.

Why don't cats play poker in the jungle?
There are too many cheetahs.

What do you call cheese that is sad?
Blue cheese.

What dog chases anything that's red?
A bulldog.

Silly Stat: Bulls (not bulldogs) have a reputation for charging when they see the color red. In fact, bulls are color-blind! It's the waving material that makes the bull charge.

What's the difference between a dog and a marine biologist?
One wags a tail and the other tags a whale.

What did the boat say to the pier?
"What's up, dock?"

Where do you find a chicken with no legs?
Anywhere you left it.

Where do cars go for a swim?
A carpool.

Why don't cats like online shopping?
They prefer a cat-alog.

What do you call blueberries playing the guitar?
A jam session.

What do you call a cat caught by the police?
A purrpetrator.

What does a grape say when it gets stepped on?
Nothing, it just lets out a little wine.

**What do teddy bears
do when it rains?**
They get wet.

**What do cats eat
for breakfast?**
Mice Krispies

What do dancing hens lay?
Scrambled eggs.

**Why do pandas like
old movies?**
They prefer black-
and-white film.

**What do camels use to
hide themselves?**
Camel-flage.

**Why did the cat run
away from the tree?**
It was scared of its bark.

**What did one toilet
say to the other?**
You look a bit flushed.

**When should you bring
your dad to school?**
When you have a Pop quiz.

**What is the richest
kind of soup?**
Won-ton soup.

Silly Stat: The Korean Republic *won* is the official paper currency of South Korea. On Seollal, the Lunar New Year, South Korean children receive crisp paper money in beautiful, colorful envelopes as a gift.

**Why shouldn't you tell
a secret on a farm?**
Because the potatoes have
eyes and the corn have ears.

**What's a cat's
favorite dessert?**
A mice-cream cone.

**What are hot dogs
called in winter?**
Chilly dogs.

**What do police officers
say to their stomachs?**
"You're under a vest."

What did the astronaut cook in his skillet?
Unidentified frying objects.

What do you get if you cross an apple with a shellfish?
A crab apple!

Silly Stat: There are a total of 7,500 varieties of apples grown around the world. Twenty-five hundred different types are grown in the United States. In the late 18th and early 19th centuries, John Chapman, better known as "Johnny Appleseed," planted apple orchards throughout Pennsylvania, Ohio, West Virginia, Illinois, and Indiana.

What do you get when you mix a duck with a firework?
A firequacker.

Why did the policeman give the sheep a ticket?
She made an illegal ewe turn.

How do cats get over a fight?
They hiss and make up.

How many apples grow on trees?
All of them.

KNOCK-KNOCK JOKES

Knock, knock.
Who's there?
Koala!
Koala who?
Koala Duty: Black Ops.

Knock, knock.
Who's there?
Fairy.
Fairy who?
**Fairy nice of you to
open the door.**

Knock, knock.
Who's there?
Peeka.
Peeka who?
Peeka-boo.

Knock, knock.
Who's there?
Jester.
Jester who?
Jester minute, I'm coming.

Silly Stat: A jester was a person hired to entertain kings, queens, and their entourages. Many of them knew how to juggle, tell jokes, and do magic tricks. They wore brightly colored clothes and funny hats. They made up silly songs, and sometimes even made fun of royalty.

Knock, knock.
Who's there?
Scold.
Scold who?
**'Scold out here. I want
to come inside!**

Knock, knock.
Who's there?
Baby.
Baby who?
**Baby shark, doo, doo,
doo, doo, doo, doo.**

Knock, knock.
Who's there?
Felix.
Felix who?
Felix-hausted. Let me in.

Knock, knock.
Who's there?
Haven.
Haven who?
**Haven you heard enough of
these knock-knock jokes?**

Knock, knock.
Who's there?
Honeydew.
Honeydew who?
Honeydew open this door, please.

Silly Stat: Watermelons, cantaloupes, and honeydew melons are made up of 90 percent water, making them perfect for quenching your thirst on a hot day!

Knock, knock.
Who's there?
Stopwatch.
Stopwatch who?
Stopwatch you are doing and answer the door!

Knock, knock.
Who's there?
Mind.
Mind who?
Mind your manners and say "hello."

Knock, knock.
Who's there?
Some.
Some who?
Somebody wants to visit you.

Knock, knock.
Who's there?
Doorway.
Doorway who?
Door weigh too much, help me open it.

Knock, knock.
Who's there?
Iran.
Iran who?
Iran all the way here to tell you.

Knock, knock.
Who's there?
Garden.
Garden who?
Garden the door from invaders!

Knock, knock.
Who's there?
Needle.
Needle who?
**Needle lil' help with
this doorknob.**

Silly Stat: Humans as far back as 12,000 years ago made needles out of animal bones, antlers, and tusks. These needles were mostly used to make fishing nets and carrying bags for the people's nomadic life. Sewing things made it possible for hunters and gatherers to carry their belongings to new territories.

Knock, knock.
Who's there?
Spin.
Spin who?
**Spin a while since I've
been here, let me in!**

Knock, knock.
Who's there?
Heart.
Heart who?
**Heart you were having
a party, let me in.**

Knock, knock.
Who's there?
Pizza.
Pizza who?
**Pizza open the door,
I'm tired of waiting.**

Knock, knock.
Who's there?
Peas.
Peas who?
**Peas open up, I have to
go to the bathroom!**

Knock, knock.
Who's there?
Oscar'd.
Oscar'd who?
**Oscar'd of the dark,
let me in.**

Knock, knock.
Who's there?
Doe.
Doe who?
Doe, a deer, a female deer.

Silly Stat: There are 60-plus species of deer worldwide. Deer are present on all continents except Antarctica and are recognized for their beautiful antlers. Antlers are the fastest-growing living tissue in the world!

Knock, knock.
Who's there?
Nine.
Nine who?
Nine of your business.

Knock, knock.
Who's there?
Take out.
Take out who?
Take out the garbage tonight, honey!

Knock, knock.
Who's there?
Red.
Red who?
Ready or not, I'm coming in.

Knock, knock.
Who's there?
Blue.
Blue who?
Don't cry. I didn't mean to startle you.

Knock, knock.
Who's there?
Juicy.
Juicy who?
Juicy me through the window?

Knock, knock.
Who's there?
The interrupting bee.
The interrupting bee who?
"Buzzzzzz."

Knock, knock.
Who's there?
Cook.
Cook who?
Cook coo! Do you hear the clock?

Knock, knock.
Who's there?
Time.
Time who?
Time to answer the door.

Knock, knock.
Who's there?
Doctor.
Doctor Who?
I like that show, too!

> **Silly Stat:** *Doctor Who* is a popular science fiction television program that has been on the air for a very long time in Britain. Doctor Who is an alien who explores the universe throughout different time periods in his spaceship. To date, there have been 13 actors who have played the character Doctor Who. The newest actor is the first woman to play the role.

Knock, knock.
Who's there?
Hawaii.
Hawaii who?
I'm fine, Hawaii you?

Knock, knock.
Who's there?
In a loop.
In a loop who?
Knock, knock.

Knock, knock.
Who's there?
House.
House who?
House you gonna know if you don't answer the door?

Knock, knock.
Who's there?
Justin.
Justin who?
Justin time to open the door.

Knock, knock.
Who's there?
Déjà.
Déjà who?
Knock, knock.

Knock, knock.
Who's there?
Mustache.
Mustache who?
**Mustache you a question,
but I'll shave it for later!**

Silly Stat: "Déjà vu" is a French term meaning "already seen." It is described as a feeling that you've experienced something once before. On average, people who report having feelings of déjà vu say it happens to them about once per year.

Knock, knock.
Who's there?
Annabel.
Annabel who?
Annabel go ring, ring.

Knock, knock.
Who's there?
Waiter.
Waiter who?
**Waiter minute,
I'm coming in.**

Knock, knock.
Who's there?
Tex.
Tex who?
**Tex me a message
and I'll tell you.**

Knock, knock.
Who's there?
Take me.
Take me who?
Take me out to the ball game.

Knock, knock.
Who's there?
Tell.
Tell who?
Tell ya later.

Knock, knock.
Who's there?
Leaf.
Leaf who?
**Leaf what you're doing
and come here.**

Will you remember
me in a year?
Yes.
Will you remember
me in a month?
Yes.
Will you remember
me in a second?
Yes!
Knock, knock.
Who's there?
You forgot me already!!!

Knock, knock.
Who's there?
Weed.
Weed who?
Weed need to open the
door to find out.

Silly Stat: Weeds
are plants that people
think are bad because
they grow, sometimes
wildly, on their own. Of
some 250,000 plant
species worldwide, only
about 3 percent behave
like unruly weeds.

Knock, knock.
Who's there?
Toupees.
Toupees who?
Toupees in a pod.

Knock, knock.
Who's there?
Jim.
Jim who?
Jim mind if I come in
to play with you?

Knock, knock.
Who's there?
Fanny.
Fanny who?
Fanny body wants to come
out, we want to play.

Knock, knock.
Who's there?
Yo.
Yo who?
Not yo *who*,
yo *ho*—it's a pirate!

Knock, knock.
Who's there?
Dash.
Dash who?
Dash a person on your
doorstep. Open the door!

Knock, knock.
Who's there?
iPad.
iPad who?
iPad for the pizza.
Gimme a slice!

Knock, knock.
Who's there?
Buh.
Buh who?
Buh-bye, I'm leaving.

Knock, knock.
Who's there?
Toll.
Toll who?
Toll you someone was
knocking at the door.

Knock, knock.
Who's there?
Common.
Common who?
Common get it.

Knock, knock.
Who's there?
Papa Bear.
Papa Bear who?
Papa Beary hungry
for porridge!

Knock, knock.
Who's there?
Snow.
Snow who?
Snow business like
show business.

Knock, knock.
Who's there?
Broom.
Broom who?
Broom, broom, it's a motorcycle.

Knock, knock.
Who's there?
Europe.
Europe who?
Europe-ning the door?

Knock, knock.
Who's there?
Ice.
Ice who?
Ice said it was me.

Knock, knock.
Who's there?
Avenue.
Avenue who?
Avenue seen it coming?

Knock, knock.
Who's there?
Says.
Says who?
Says me, that's who.

Knock, knock.
Who's there?
Pasta.
Pasta who?
Pasta la vista, baby.

Knock, knock.
Who's there?
Omar.
Omar who?
**Omar goodness gracious,
you forgot I was visiting you.**

Knock, knock.
Who's there?
Aaron.
Aaron who?
**Aaron you gonna open
the door and find out?**

Knock, knock.
Who's there?
Shiz.
Shiz-who?
**Yes, I'm looking for
my little dog!**

Silly Stat: Shih tzus are a type of dog that originated from the country Tibet. Their name means "Little Lion." They were often given as gifts to the emperors of China.

Knock, knock.
Who's there?
Dewey.
Dewey who?
**Dewey have to keep doing
knock-knock jokes?**

Knock, knock.
Who's there?
Howl.
Howl who?
**Howl you know unless
you open the door?**

Knock, knock.
Who's there?
Heidi.
Heidi who?
**Heidi who, hidey
ho, neighbor!**

Knock, knock.
Who's there?
Police.
Police who?
Police let me in, already.

Knock, knock.
Who's there?
Yah.
Yah who?
Nah, I like Google better.

Knock, knock.
Who's there?
Hike.
Hike who?
**I didn't know you liked
Japanese poetry!**

Silly Stat: Haiku are short poems that follow a brief syllable pattern, such as 5-7-5 or 3-5-3. The poems originated in Japan. Here's an example:

Jokes slip from the tongue
To fill the heart with humor
Laughter soothes the soul

Knock, knock.
Who's there?
To.
To who?
It's "to whom."

Knock, knock.
Who's here?
Wendy.
Wendy who?
Wendy bell gonna get fixed?

Knock, knock.
Who's there?
Iva.
Iva who?
**Iva sore hand from
all this knocking.**

Knock, knock.
Who's there?
Otto.
Otto who?
Otto know either, do you?

Knock, knock.
Who's there?
Shamp.
Shamp who?
**Thanks, my hair was
kind of dirty!**

Knock, knock.
Who's there?
Roach.
Roach who?
**Roach you a text,
didn't you read it?**

Knock-knock.
Who's there?
Tune-y.
Tune-y who?
Tune-y fish.

Knock, knock.
Who's there?
Iron.
Iron who?
Iron the right to run free!

Knock, knock.
Who's there?
Chick.
Chick who?
**Chick the peephole
and you'll find out.**

Knock, knock.
Who's there?
'Sup.
'Sup who?
'Sup, buttercup?

Knock, knock.
Who's there?
Amanda.
Amanda who?
Amanda fix your doorbell.

Knock, knock.
Who's there?
Nicholas.
Nicholas who?
A Nicholas not much money these days.

Knock, knock.
Who's there?
Candice.
Candice who?
Candice be the last knock-knock joke?

Knock, knock.
Who's there.
Jada.
Jada who?
Jada say the word and I'll stop.

Knock, knock.
Who's there?
Nuisance.
Nuisance who?
What's nuisance yesterday?

Knock, knock.
Who's there?
Dolphin.
Dolphin who?
Dolphin make no difference, open the door.

Silly Stat: Dolphins live in groups that hunt and play together. Large groups of dolphins are called "pods" and can have 1,000 members or more. Dolphins are carnivores. Fish, squid, and crustaceans are included in their diet. A 260-pound dolphin eats about 33 pounds of fish a day.

Knock, knock.
Who's there?
Asparagus.
Asparagus who?
Asparagus doesn't have a last name.

Knock, knock.
Who's there?
Goliath.
Goliath who?
**Goliath down, thou
look-eth tired!**

Knock, knock.
Who's there?
An extraterrestrial.
An extraterrestrial who?
**Wait, how many
extraterrestrials
do you know?!**

Knock, knock.
Who's there?
Control Freak.
Con—
**Okay, now you say,
"Control Freak who?!"**

Knock, knock.
Who's there?
Snow.
Snow who?
**Snow use. I forgot
my name again!**

Knock, knock.
Who's there?
Closure.
Closure who?
**Closure book and
open the door!**

Knock, knock.
Who's there?
Ho-ho.
Ho-ho who?
**You know, your Santa
impression could
use a little work.**

Knock, knock.
Who's there?
Aiden Snufflemount.
Aiden Snufflemount who?
**Oh, come on, how many
"Aiden Snufflemounts"
do you know?**

Knock, knock.
Who's there?
Rhino.
Rhino who?
**Rhino every knock-knock
joke there is!**

Knock, knock.
Who's there?
Witches.
Witches who?
**Witches the way
to the movies?**

Knock, knock.
Who's there?
Ice-Cream Soda.
Ice-Cream Soda who?
Ice-Cream Soda whole
neighborhood can hear!

Knock, knock.
Who's there?
Zany.
Zany who?
Zanybody home?

Knock, knock.
Who's there?
Jess.
Jess who?
Jess open the door.

Knock, knock.
Who's there?
Noise.
Noise who?
Noise to see you!

Knock, knock.
Who's there?
Conrad.
Conrad who?
Conrad-ulations! That was
a good knock-knock joke.

Knock, knock.
Who's there?
Razor.
Razor who?
Razor hands and dance
through the doorway!

Knock, knock.
Who's there?
Bruce.
Bruce who?
I Bruce easily, my fingers
are stuck in the door!

Knock, knock.
Who's there?
Ears.
Ears who?
Ears another knock-knock
joke for you!

Knock, knock.
Who's there?
Ferdie!
Ferdie who?
Ferdie last time—
open this door!

Knock, knock.
Who's there?
Keanu.
Keanu who?
Keanu let me in,
it's cold out here.

Knock, knock.
Who's there?
Claire.
Claire who?
**Claire the doorway,
I'm coming in!**

Knock, knock.
Who's there?
Nobel.
Nobel who?
Nobel, so I guess I'll knock.

Knock, knock.
Who's there?
Value.
Value who?
Value be my Valentine?

Knock, knock.
Who's there.
Amish.
Amish who?
Amish you so much!

Knock, knock.
Who's there?
Howie.
Howie who?
**Howie gonna get
in the house?**

Knock, knock.
Who's there?
Theodore.
Theodore who?
Theodore between us.

Knock, knock.
Who's there?
Grandma.
Grandma who?
Knock, knock.
Who's there?
Grandma.
Grandma who?
Knock, knock.
Who's there?
Aunt.
Aunt who?
**Aunt you glad I didn't
say "Grandma"?**

Knock, knock.
Who's there?
Toby.
Toby who?
**Toby or not to be?
That is the question.**

Knock, knock.
Who's there?
Wire.
Wire who?
Wire you asking me that?

Knock, knock.
Who's there?
Owl.
Owl who?
Owl aboard!

Knock, knock.
Who's there?
Weirdo.
Weirdo who?
**Weirdo you think
you're going?**

Knock, knock.
Who's there?
Wood ant.
Wood ant who?
**Wood ant be knocking if I
didn't need to come inside.**

Knock, knock.
Who's there?
Cozy.
Cozy who?
**Cozy who's knocking
at the door.**

Knock, knock.
Who's there?
Baby owl.
Baby Owl who?
**Baby Owl use the back
door next time.**

Knock, knock.
Who's there?
R2.
R2 who?
R2-D2.

Knock, knock.
Who's there?
Safari.
Safari who?
Sa-fari, so good.

Knock, knock.
Who's there?
2:30.
2:30 who?
**I made an appointment
with the dentist because
my 2:30 (tooth-hurty).**

Knock, knock.
Who's there?
Gopher.
Gopher who?
**Gopher some ice
cream together?**

Knock, knock.
Who's there?
Herring.
Herring who?
**Herring some terrible
knock-knock jokes!**

Knock, knock.
Who's there?
Who.
Who who?
Sorry, I don't speak owl!

Knock, knock.
Who's there?
Nota.
Nota who?
**Nota 'nother
knock-knock joke.**

Knock, knock.
Who's there?
Rita.
Rita who?
**Rita note and then
you'll know.**

Knock, knock.
Who's there?
Pasture.
Pasture who?
**Pasture bedtime, but
I'm knocking anyway.**

Knock, knock.
Who's there?
Waiter.
Waiter who?
**Waiter minute, I have
to put on my jacket.**

Knock, knock.
Who's there?
Geese.
Geese who?
I'm not telling you!

Knock, knock.
Who's there?
Tish.
Tish who?
**Tish-who for your
runny nose?**

Knock, knock.
Who's there?
Radio.
Radio who?
Radio not, here I come.

Knock, knock.
Who's there?
Kenya.
Kenya who?
Kenya feel the love tonight?

Knock, knock.
Who's there?
Yetta.
Yetta who?
**Yetta 'nother
knock-knock joke.**

Knock, knock.
Who's there?
Armenia.
Armenia who?
Armenia every word I say!

Knock, knock.
Who's there?
Butcher.
Butcher who?
**Butcher left leg in,
butcher left leg out!**

Knock, knock.
Who's there?
Surgeon.
Surgeon who?
Surgeon thou shalt find.

Silly Stat: Old English is one of the first forms of the English language. It was used from 450 CE to 1100 CE throughout England. It sounds a little bit like German. It is very different from the English we speak today!

Knock, knock.
Who's there?
Heart.
Heart who?
**Heart you the first
time, don't yell!**

Knock, knock.
Who's there?
Wood.
Wood who?
**Wood you do me a favor
and open the door?**

Knock, knock.
Who's there?
**R-U-N. (Hint: read the
letters, not the whole word.)**
R-U-N who?
R-U-N the car yet?

Knock, knock.
Who's there?
Ooze!
Ooze who?
Ooze in charge around here?

Knock, knock.
Who's there?
Letter.
Letter who?
**Letter in or she'll knock
down the door!**

Knock, knock.
Who's there?
Sweden.
Sweden who?
Sweden sour chicken!

Knock, knock.
Who's there?
Icing.
Icing who?
**Icing so loudly that
everyone can hear me!**

Knock, knock.
Who's there?
Godiva.
Godiva who?
**Godiva terrible headache,
do you have an aspirin?**

Knock, knock.
Who's there?
Handsome.
Handsome who?
**Handsome sunscreen
over, the sun is blazing!**

Knock, knock.
Who's there?
Nuff.
Nuff who?
**Nuff knock-knock
jokes, please.**

Knock, knock.
Who's there?
Dishes.
Dishes who?
**Dishes the last
knock-knock joke.**

TONGUE TWISTERS

**Many mumbling mice are making
merry music in the moonlight.**

Truly rural.

Specific Pacific.

Selfish shellfish.

Silly Stat: Lobsters taste with their legs and chew with their stomachs. Their nervous system is similar to those of grasshoppers and ants. Sometimes they are called "bugs."

Silly sushi chef.

Six silly socks.

Daddy draws doors.

Shine so shiny.

Ed had edited it.

She saw Sam.

She shifts sheep.

Willie's really weary.

Wren rents right.

She steals cheese.

Bake big batches.

Fresh fried fish.

World Wide Web.

Blue box hot ox.

Two twirled 'til ten.

Octopus ocular optics.

Friendly fleas and fireflies.

Zebras zig and zebras zag.

Raw wretched rain runs.

Fred fed four frogs.

Wanda watches whales
on Wednesdays.

Buck bought burros best.

> **Silly Stat:** "*Burro*" is the Spanish word for "donkey." Donkeys have incredibly strong memories. They can recognize areas they haven't seen for up to 25 years!

Susie sits silver seats.

Rubber baby buggy bumpers.

Cooks cook cupcakes quickly.

The blue bluebird blinks.

Still sell silk shirts.

Ralph rode red roadsters.

Six slimy snails
sailed silently.

Quick kiss, quick
kiss, quick kiss.

Pad kid poured curd
pulled cod.

She threw three free throws.

Shave a single shingle thin.

Fetch four fine fresh fish.

Green glass globes
gently glowing.

A snake sneaks to seek a snack.

Nine nimble newts
nibbling nuts.

Not these things here,
but those things there.

She should shun
the shining sun.

Silly Stat: The world's oldest chewing gum is 9,000 years old. Many old civilizations enjoyed the pastime of chewing gum. The ancient Greeks chewed *mastic*, whereas the ancient Mayan Indians were busy chomping on *chicle*.

Tim threw three
thumbtacks.

She fed six sheep cheap chow.

Twelve twins
twirled 12 twigs.

Thinkers thinking thick
thoughtful thoughts.

We shall surely see
the sunshine soon.

I like New York, unique New
York, I like unique New York.

Two tiny timid toads trying
to trot to Tarrytown.

Lucky rabbits revel
in ruckus.

Silly Stat: The big
difference between
frogs and toads is
that frogs need to live
near water to survive,
whereas toads do not.
Toads have drier, wart-
covered, leathery skin
and shorter legs than
frogs. That's why some
species of toads can be
found in deserts, where
water is hard to find.

Silly Stat: A female
rabbit is called a "doe."
A male rabbit is called a
"buck." A young rabbit is
called a "kit." More than
half of the world's rabbits
live in North America.

I looked right at Larry's
rally and left in a hurry.

I wish to wash my
wristwatch.

Three gray geese in
green fields grazing.

Wrecked sets right
where you went.

Two towels tossed
toward toes.

Four furious friends
fought for the phone.

A really leery Larry rolls
readily to the road.

I saw a sight; the
sight saw me.

Rory's lawn rake rarely
rakes really right.

Night nurses nursing
nicely nightly.

Watch right, right watch.

The big bug bit the
little beetle.

Silly Stat: Beetles live
everywhere. Did you
know that one out of
every four animals on
Earth is a beetle? Most
adult beetles wear
shells like body armor
and can vary in size.
The largest beetle, a
Titanus giganteus, can
grow up to six and a
half inches in size!

The cat catchers can't
catch caught cats.

Little Lillian lets lazy lizards
lie along the lily pads.

Fred fed Ted bread, and
Ted fed Fred bread.

A bragging baker
baked black bread.

Silly Stat: In London,
fire broke out at Thomas
Farriner's bakery on
Pudding Lane a little
after midnight on
Sunday, September 2,
1666. The fire destroyed
some 13,200 homes,
plus 84 churches
and other important
buildings such as
the Royal Exchange,
Guildhall, and St. Paul's
Cathedral. More than
100,000 people were left
homeless. But one good
thing came out of the
fire: It destroyed most of
the rats infecting people
with the plague, stopping
the deadly disease!

Send toast to ten tense
temps in ten tall tents.

Three fluffy feathers fell
from Phyllis's flimsy fan.

Each Easter Eddie eats
80 Easter eggs.

I saw Sherry sitting in
a shoeshine shop.

On a lazy laser raiser
lies a laser ray eraser.

Silly Stat: The word
"laser" is actually an
acronym for "light
amplification by
stimulated emission of
radiation." The strength
of early lasers was
measured in Gillettes
(yes, like the razor!). In
1960, Theodore Maiman
measured the strength
of a laser by the number
of razor blades a beam
could cut through.

If cows could fly, I'd have
a cow pie in my eye.

Lions loan lots of
lottery letters lately.

"Surely Sylvia swims!"
shrieked Sammy, surprised.

The boot band brought
the black boot back.

Vincent vowed vengeance
very vehemently.

Letty lets lovely
levers level lazily.

A skunk sat on a stump and thunk the stump
stunk, but the stump thunk the skunk stunk.

How much pot could a
pot roast roast, if a pot
roast could roast pot?

Betty and Bob brought
back blue balloons
from the big bazaar.

Silly stat: Balloons
galore! Did you know
that before toy balloons
were invented, people
made balloons by
inflating pig bladders
and animal intestines?
Later came the hot-air
balloon created by the
Montgolfier brothers,
which was designed
to help people travel
by flight. The brothers
launched a giant balloon
with a passenger basket
on November 21, 1783.

How many yaks could
a yak pack pack if a yak
pack could pack yaks?

Six sheep sleep on silk sheets.

Pat the fat black cat
on the back.

If there never was an ever,
then the ever was not never.

How can a clam cram in
a clean cream can?

Ryan ran rings around
the Roman ruins.

If Stu chews shoes,
should Stu choose the
shoes he chews?

Six sick chicks nick six slick
bricks with picks and sticks.

Don't be late at the gate for
our date at a quarter to eight.

Lesser leather never
weathered wetter
weather better.

I saw a saw that could
out-saw any other
saw I ever saw.

Does your sport shop stock
short socks with spots?

Rory the warrior and Roger the worrier read rapidly in rural Raleigh.

A tricky, frisky shrimp with sixty super scaly stripes sips soapy soda in the slick sunshine.

Any noise annoys an oyster, but a noisy noise annoys an oyster more.

Silly Stat: Oysters grow on reefs that provide a natural barrier to storm waves and rising sea levels. They absorb as much as 76 to 93 percent of wave energy, which reduces erosion, flooding, and property damage when there are coastal storms like hurricanes. Oyster reefs are in great danger from overfishing and pollution.

A big bug bit the little beetle but the little beetle bit the big bug back.

If you notice this notice, you will notice that this notice is not worth notice.

I am not a pheasant-plucker, but a pheasant-plucker's son. And I am only plucking pheasants 'til the pheasant-plucker comes.

If two witches were watching two watches, which witch would watch which watch?

Swan swam over the sea—swim, swan, swim! Swan swam back again—well swum, swan!

If you must cross a coarse, cross cow across a crowded cow-crossing, cross the cross, coarse cow across the crowded cow-crossing carefully.

Puns & One-Liners

What's Moby Dick's favorite dinner?
Fish and *ships.*

Currently, the flower business is *blooming*.

You have cat to be *kitten me right meow*.

The best way to communicate with fish is to *drop them a line*.

Let *minnow* what you think.

> **Silly Stat:** The term "minnow" describes any small, silvery fish. Most species of minnows are less than four inches in length and have a relatively short life span of three to four years. Larger minnow varieties can live for up to 10 years.

What is every whale's favorite greeting?
Whale hello there!

What did the lawyer name his daughter?
Sue.

What did the hamburger name its baby?
Patty!

When is a tire a bad singer?
When it's *flat*.

Why do bees hum?
They don't know *the words*.

Never tell a bald guy a *hair-raising* story.

I wrote a song about a tortilla.
Well actually, it's more of a *wrap*.

Why are eggs not into jokes?
Because they could *crack up*.

What's a chicken's favorite vegetable?
Eggplant.

This gravity joke is getting a bit old, but I *fall for it* every time.

Want to go on a picnic?
Alpaca lunch.

Silly Stat: Alpacas were domesticated by the Incas in South America more than 6,000 years ago and raised for their beautiful wool. Alpaca fiber is much like sheep's wool, but warmer and not itchy. Most people find they are not allergic to it. Because of their calm and gentle nature, alpacas are used in some countries as therapy animals.

If you need help building an ark, I *Noah* guy.

How do trees get online? They just *log in.*

Why was the chef arrested? She was *beating the eggs.*

Pencils could be made with erasers at both ends, but what would be *the point*?

He wears glasses during math because it improves *division.*

I wasn't originally going to get a brain transplant, but then I *changed my mind.*

Don't spell "part" backward. It's a *trap.*

I'm reading a book about gravity. It's impossible to *put down.*

Don't trust atoms, they *make up* everything.

What do you call the security outside of a Samsung store? Guardians of the Galaxy.

I accidentally handed my brother a glue stick instead of a ChapStick. He still isn't talking to me.

When I lose the TV controller, it's always hidden in some *remote* location.

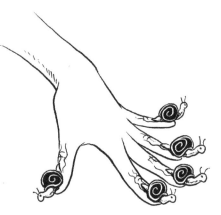

Where do you find *giant snails*? On the ends of giants' fingers.

Did you hear about the *kidnapping* at school? It's okay, he woke up.

RIP, boiled water. You will be mist.

My teacher told me to "have a good day," so I *went home.*

Why do dragons sleep all day?
They like to hunt *knights*.

Silly Stat: Dragons are mythical creatures written about in the folklore of many cultures since the beginning of civilization. Dragons generally have reptilian characteristics and can be helpful and guardian-like, although others are vicious and deadly. When the first dinosaur bones were discovered years ago, people thought the large bones were those of dragons.

Did you hear about the
new auto body shop?
It comes highly
wreck-a-mended.

What sound does a
sleeping T. rex make?
A *dino-snore*.

I'm glad I know sign
language, it's pretty *handy*.

> **Silly Stat:** Sign
> language varies around
> the world. Even in the
> same country, sign
> language can have
> different dialects or
> ways of speaking.
> In North America,
> people use American
> Sign Language.

How much money does
a pirate pay for corn?
A *buccaneer.*

Don't interrupt your
mother when she is
working on a puzzle.
You'll hear some *crosswords.*

Did you hear that the
coin factory closed
down yesterday?
It doesn't make any *cents.*

Have you ever heard of
an honest *cheetah?*

> **Silly stat:** When
> cheetahs are running at
> full speed, their stride
> (length between steps)
> is six to seven meters, or
> about 21 feet. Their feet
> only the touch ground
> twice during each stride.

Knowing how to pick
locks has really *opened
a lot of doors* for me.

A friend wanted to have a
contest with bird puns, but
toucan play that game.

If a wild pig kills you,
does it mean you've been
boared to death?

How did the turkey win the talent show?
With its *drumsticks.*

Vegans believe meat eaters and butchers are gross. But those who sell you fruit and vegetables are *grocer.*

Jokes about unemployed people are not funny. They just *don't work*.

Did you hear police arrested the World Tongue Twister Champion? I imagine he'll be given a *tough sentence.*

Why is Peter Pan always flying? He *neverlands.*

What did the librarian say when the books were in a mess? We ought to be ashamed of *our shelves*!

What do baseball players eat on? Home plates!

What do you call a musician with problems? A *trebled* man.

What's an avocado's favorite music? *Guac* 'n' roll.

Silly Stat: Did you know that avocados are a fruit and not a vegetable? Avocados are an Aztec symbol of love and fertility because they grow in pairs on trees. Avocados are not only the main ingredient in guacamole and an addition to sandwiches and salads; in some places, such as Brazil, people also add avocados to ice cream!

What do you call a musical cow? A *moo*-sician.

I've started sleeping in our fireplace. Now I sleep like a *log*!

What's a golf club's favorite type of music? Swing.

Someone sent 10 different puns to friends, with the hope that at least one of the puns would make them laugh.
No pun *in 10* did.

I'm going to buy some Velcro for my shoes instead of laces.
Why *knot*?

Did you hear about the new gym that shut down?
It just didn't **work out.**

Why did the pianist keep banging his head against the keys?
He was playing *by ear.*

Did you hear about the boy who tried to catch fog?
He *mist.*

I went to a seafood disco last week and pulled a *mussel.*

Long fairy tales have a tendency to *dragon.*

Why was the teacher cross-eyed?
Her **pupils** got out of control.

Peacocks are meticulous because they show attention to *de tail.*

Silly Stat: Technically, only male peafowl are called "peacocks." Female peafowl are referred to as "peahens." Babies are called "peachicks." Male peachicks don't start growing their showy trains until about age three, but a full-grown peacock's tail feathers can reach up to six feet long and make up about 60 percent of its body's length. Despite their large size, peacocks do fly.

What did the dolphin say after he accidentally swam into another sea creature?
I didn't do it on porpoise.

What is Beethoven
doing now?
De-composing.

Silly Stat: German
composer Ludwig
van Beethoven is
known for creating
nine symphonies, five
concertos for the piano,
32 piano sonatas, and
16 string quartets. He
also composed other
chamber music, choral
works, and songs, all
while losing his hearing.
By the time he was
31, Beethoven had
lost 60 percent of his
hearing. Eventually,
he went totally deaf.

Somebody stole
all my lamps.
I couldn't be more *de-lighted!*

Who is the penguin's
favorite aunt?
Aunt-Arctica!

Did you hear about the
skunk that fell in the river?
It *stank* to the bottom.

Why did the chicken
cross the playground?
To get to the other *slide.*

Isn't it scary that doctors call
what they do *"practice"*?

Hung a picture up on
the wall the other day.
Nailed it.

Did you hear about the two
antennas who met on a roof,
fell in love, and got married?
The ceremony wasn't
much, but the reception
was excellent.

What is brown, hairy,
and wears sunglasses?
A coconut on vacation.

The cats not feline well?
Call a *purrimedic.*

How do construction
workers party?
They raise the *roof.*

I told my mom that I was going
to make a bike out of spaghetti.
You should have seen her face
when I rode **straight pasta.**

How does a gorilla
ring the doorbell?
King Kong! King Kong!

Did you hear about the
angry bird that landed
on a doorknob?
It really flew *off the handle*.

What days do mothers
have baby boys?
Son-days.

I broke my finger yesterday.
On the other hand, I'm okay.

What did the buffalo
say when his son went
off to college?
"Bison."

If you spent your day in
a well, can you say your
day was *well-spent*?

What sort of TV shows
do ducks watch?
*Duck*umentaries.

What did the dad spider
say to the baby spider?
You spend too much
time on the *web*.

If you're scared of
elevators, start taking
steps to avoid them.

Some people say I'm
addicted to somersaults,
but that's just *how I roll*.

I was hoping to steal some
leftovers from the party, but
I guess my plans were *foiled*.

Silly Stat: The United
States first produced
aluminum foil in 1913
to use in making
identification leg bands
for racing pigeons! That
same year, Life Savers
was founded and began
wrapping its Pep O Mint
candies in tinfoil to
keep them fresh.

What's the worst part about movie theater candy prices? They're always *Raisinet*.

Silly Stat: The first official permanent movie theater was located on Main Street in Buffalo, New York. It was opened on Monday, October 19, 1896, by Thomas Edison. It seated more than 70 people. At the time, the theater showed mostly travel films, but people were amazed to see moving pictures on a large screen!

Did you hear about the guy who was admitted to the hospital with a horse in his stomach? Don't worry, his condition is *stable*.

When a new hive is done, bees have a house-*swarming* party.

I went to buy some camouflage pants the other day, but I *couldn't find any*.

My roommates are concerned that I'm using their kitchen utensils, but that's a *whisk* I'm willing to take.

Did you hear about the woman who sued the airport for misplacing her luggage? She *lost* her case.

How can you tell if a vampire has a cold? He starts *coffin*.

My uncle bought a donkey because he thought he might get a *kick out of* it.

In the winter my dog wears his coat, but in the summer, he wears his coat and *pants*.

Thanks for explaining the word "many" to me; *it means a lot*.

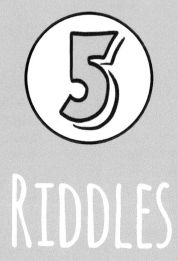

RIDDLES

Riddles can be hoot-hollerin' funny. And sometimes, they're so tricky they're a joke! Can you scratch your noggin and solve the following riddles?

(Answers are on page 140.)

1. What is as big as an elephant,
but weighs nothing at all?

2. The more you take away, the larger it becomes. What is it?

3. What has many rings, but no fingers?

4. What five-letter word becomes shorter when you add two letters to it?

5. Why would a man living in New York not be buried in Chicago?

Silly Stat: The Willis Tower (formerly known as "Sears Tower") is one of Chicago's most popular tourist attractions. It is the third-tallest building in the Western Hemisphere. On a clear day, visitors can see four states from the Skydeck: Illinois, Indiana, Wisconsin, and Michigan.

6. What can honk without a horn?

7. What has a horn but doesn't honk?

8. What's a 10-letter word that starts with gas?

9. You can you serve it, but never eat it. What is it?

10. What kind of coat can you only put on when it is wet?

11. What flies around all day but never goes anywhere?

12. What ship has two mates, but no captain?

13. Which candles burn longer, tallow or beeswax?

14. What is only a small box but can weigh over a hundred pounds?

15. What travels around the world but stays in one spot?

16. Why would a baby ant be confused when he looks at his family?

17. What always sleeps with its shoes on?

18. I am a word. If you pronounce me right, it will be wrong. If you pronounce me wrong, it will be right. What word am I?

19. A farmer has 10 chickens, five horses, two children, and a wife. How many feet are on the farm?

20. A taxi driver is going the wrong way down a one-way street. He passes four police officers, but none of them stop him. Why?

21. Mr. Blue lives in the Blue House. Mrs. Yellow lives in the Yellow House. Mr. Orange lives in the Orange House. Who lives in the White House?

Silly Stat: At various times throughout history, the White House has been known as the "President's Palace," the "President's House," and the "Executive Mansion." President Theodore Roosevelt officially gave the White House its current name in 1901. In the White House, there are 412 doors, 147 windows, 28 fireplaces, eight staircases, and three elevators.

22. You can hear it, but you can't touch or see it. It is unique to you, but everyone has one. What is it?

23. They come out at night without being called. They are lost during the day without being stolen. What are they?

24. There were five people under an umbrella. Why didn't they get wet?

Silly Stat: The word "umbrella" comes from the Latin word "*umbros*," which means "shade" or "shadow." The first use of umbrellas was as a parasol, to protect people from the sun.

25. Why would a boy bury his flashlight?

Silly Stat: A 2,200-year-old clay jar found near Baghdad, Iraq, has been loosely described as the oldest-known electric battery in existence. This ancient technology was discovered at a Mesopotamian archaeological dig.

26. I appear where there is light, but if a light shines on me, I disappear. What am I?

27. What seven letters did Sophie say when she saw the refrigerator had no food?

28. What happens once in a lifetime, twice in a moment, but never in one hundred years?

29. If April showers bring May flowers, what do Mayflowers bring?

30. I can be shaped, but never come free. I drive people crazy for the love of me. What am I?

31. What do you call a man who does not have all his fingers on one hand?

32. A woman is 20 years old, but only had five birthdays in her life. How?

33. What is put on a table and cut, but is never eaten?

Silly Stat: There are 52 cards in a standard deck. There are 52 weeks in a year, and if you add up all the symbols in a deck of cards, plus a "1" for each joker, the sum equals the number of days in a leap year: 366.

34. I have no life, but I can die; what am I?

35. You walk into a room with a match, a kerosene lamp, a candle, and a fireplace. What do you light first?

36. I'm always on the table for dinner, but you don't get to eat me. What am I?

37. What do you find in water that never gets wet?

38. What is easy to lift, but hard to throw?

39. What has two heads, four eyes, six legs, and a tail?

40. Why is the Mississippi such an unusual river?

41. What can go up the chimney when down, but cannot go down the chimney when up?

42. What word contains 26 letters, but only has three syllables?

43. What has a bottom at the top of it?

44. Forward I am heavy, but backward I am not. What am I?

45. What is at the end of everything?

46. The more you take, the more you leave behind. What are they?

47. A lawyer, a plumber, and a hatmaker walk down the street. Who has the biggest hat?

48. Three doctors said that Bill is their brother. Bill says he has no brothers. How many brothers does Bill actually have?

49. A little girl goes to the store and buys one dozen eggs. As she goes home, all but three break. How many eggs are left unbroken?

50. A girl fell off a 20-foot ladder. She wasn't hurt. Why?

51. I go around all of the cities, towns, and villages, but never come inside. What am I?

52. A man leaves home and turns left three times, only to return home facing two men wearing masks. Who are those two men?

53. What English word begins and ends with the same three letters?

54. People make me, save me, change me, and raise me. What am I?

55. What three letters turn a child into an adult?

56. What is higher without a head than it is with it?

57. What comes down, but never goes up?

Bonus Math Riddle!
Can you write down eight eights so that they add up to one thousand?

58. You find me in December, but not any other month. What am I?

59. What bet can never be won?

60. A word in this sentence is misspelled. What word is it?

61. I can be broken, but I never move. I can be closed and opened. I am sealed by hands. What am I?

62. I am often following you and copying your every move. Yet you can never touch me or catch me. What am I?

63. A man describes his daughters by saying, "They are all blonde but two, all brunette but two, and all redheaded but two." How many daughters does he have?

64. What type of dress can never be worn?

65. What four-letter word can be written forward, backward, or upside down, and can still be read from left to right?

66. I have hundreds of limbs but cannot walk. What am I?

67. I don't have eyes, ears, a nose, or a tongue, but I can see, smell, hear, and taste everything. What am I?

68. What cannot speak or hear anything, but always tells the truth?

Silly Stat: Some mirrors can reflect sound waves as well as reflect images. These mirrors are known as acoustic mirrors. Before the development of radar, mirrors were used in World War II to detect sounds coming from enemy aircraft.

69. What fruit can you use to sip water?

70. What has bark, but no bite?

71. I am a word of letters three; add two and fewer there will be. What word am I?

72. What can clap without any hands?

73. What word is pronounced the same if you take away four of its five letters?

74. If you drop me I'm sure to crack, but give me a smile and I'll always smile back. What am I?

75. What is black when you buy it, red when you use it, and gray when you throw it away?

76. I turn once; what is out will not get in. I turn again; what is in will not get out. What am I?

77. How does the kid cross the river without getting wet?

78. What is in the middle of the sky?

79. You can break me without touching or seeing me. What am I?

80. What wears a jacket, but no pants?

Silly Stat: Bill Gates bought the Codex Leicester, a collection of scientific writings by artist and scientist Leonardo da Vinci, for more than $30 million!

81. Take away my first letter, and I still sound the same. Take away my last letter, I still sound the same. Even take away my letter in the middle, I will still sound the same. I am a five-letter word. What am I?

82. It has eyes that cannot see, a tongue that cannot taste, and a soul that cannot die. What is it?

83. What has its heart in its head?

84. You can keep it only after giving it away to someone. What is it?

85. It has been around for millions of years but is no more than a month old. What is it?

86. What hangs all day and burns all night?

87. What loses its head in the morning, but gets it back at night?

Silly Stat: Scientists say the moon was made when a rock smashed into Earth. The most widely accepted explanation is that the moon was created when a rock the size of Mars slammed into Earth, shortly after the solar system began forming about 4.5 billion years ago. Currently, the moon is drifting away from Earth. It is moving approximately 3.8 centimeters away from our planet every year.

88. What is round on both sides but high in the middle?

89. What can point in every direction, but can't reach the destination by itself?

90. What type of cheese is made backward?

Silly Stat: Edam is a slightly hard cheese that first came from the Netherlands. It is named after a town called Edam, located in North Holland. Look for its waxy red rind in the grocery store.

91. How do you spell "mousetrap"?

92. What runs all day but never gets anywhere?

93. What goes up and down, but never moves?

94. What goes in and around the house but never touches it?

95. What match can't you put in a matchbox?

96. I babble but I can't talk. What am I?

97. I make two people out of one. What am I?

98. Take one out and scratch my head; I am now black but was once yellow and red. What am I?

99. Where do four queens stay when they are not in a castle?

100. With pointed fangs, I sit and wait. With piercing force, I snap my bait. What am I?

Silly Stat: The first known stapler was made in the 18th century in France for King Louis XV. Legend has it that the staples were made from gold, encrusted with precious stones, and bore his Royal Court's insignia. The growing use of paper in the 19th century created a demand for an efficient paper fastener. Modern staplers can be traced to a patent filed by Henry R. Heyl in Philadelphia, in 1877.

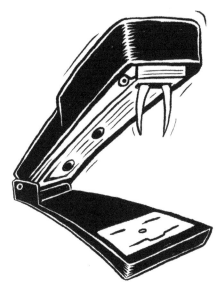

101. What part of London is in Brazil?

102. What has a neck and no head, two arms and no hands?

103. As I went across the bridge, I met a man with a load of wood, which was neither straight nor crooked. What kind of wood was it?

104. I am the mightiest weapon, but I've never fired a shot. What am I?

105. What breaks yet never falls, and what falls yet never breaks?

106. I saw an unusual book. The foreword comes after the epilogue. The end is in the first half of the book. The index comes before the introduction. Name that book.

107. I am so simple, I can only point. Yet I guide men all over the world. What am I?

108. What man cannot live in a house?

109. We are twins. We are close together, but we don't touch. We are far apart, yet we become one. What are we?

110. A house of wood in a hidden place, built without nails or glue. High above the ground, I hold something precious. What am I?

111. I can sizzle like bacon, but am made with an egg. I have plenty of backbone but lack a leg. I peel layers like an onion, but still remain whole. I'm long like a flagpole yet fit in a hole. What am I?

> **Bonus Math Riddle!**
> If 11 plus two equals 1, 9 plus five equals what?

112. I'm never thirsty, but I always drink. What am I?

113. A frog jumped into a pot of cream and started treading. It soon felt something solid under its feet. How was the frog able to hop out?

114. A horse is on a 24-foot chain and wants an apple that is 26 feet away. How did the horse reach the apple?

115. Dead on the field lie 10 soldiers in white, knocked down by three eyes, dark as night. What happened?

Silly Stat: Bowling is a very old game and dates as far back as 3200 BCE in Ancient Egypt. Modern bowling is a few thousand years younger: Indoor bowling lanes opened up in 1840 in New York City, but only men bowled at the time. Women were not allowed to bowl until 1917!

116. Turn me on my spine, open me up, and you'll be the wisest of all time. Who am I?

117. I have both face and tail, but I am not alive. Who am I?

118. I can seize and hold the wind. My touch brings giggles. Who am I?

119. The wise humans are sure of it. Even the fools know it. The rich want it. The greatest of heroes fear it. Yet the lowliest of cowards would die for it. What is it?

120. Through wind and rain, I love to play. I roam the earth, yet here I stay. I can crumble stones, and fire cannot burn me. Yet I am soft, and you can dent me with your hand. Who am I?

121. Flesh as red as blood with a heart of stone. What am I?

122. A girl is sitting in a house at night that has no lights on at all. There is no lamp, no candle, nothing to brighten the room. Yet, she is reading. How?

123. It lives in winter, dies in summer, and grows down with its roots on top. What is it?

124. How can somebody walk for eight days without sleeping?

125. You had 20 people build your house in two months. How long would it take 10 people to build the very same house?

126. I have 100 legs but cannot stand. A long neck but no head. What am I?

127. Remove the outside, cook the inside, eat the outside, throw away the inside. What am I?

128. What common English verb becomes its own past tense by rearranging its letters?

129. If you have a cube, each edge two inches long, how many total square inches are there on all eight sides?

130. Is it correct to say, "the yolk of eggs is white" or "the yolk of eggs are white"?

131. Is it legal for a man to marry his widow's sister?

132. I have no sword, I have no spear, yet rule a horde that many fear. My soldiers fight with wicked sting, I rule with might, yet am no king. What am I?

133. My forks are here; my forks are there. They're not on the table, but still everywhere. What am I?

134. What peels like an onion but still remains whole?

135. When is it bad luck to meet a white cat?

136. A farmer has 20 sheep, 10 pigs, and 10 cows. If we call the pigs cows, how many cows will he have?

137. As clear as diamonds, polished like glass. Try to keep me, and I vanish fast. What am I?

138. I soar without wings; I see without eyes. I traveled the universe and live where dreams lie. I've conquered the world, yet I'm always home. My ideas are untamed but want to be grown. What am I?

139. I am not alive, yet I can stand up. I begin as one color and then change rather abrupt. So fragile, a child could break one, yet strong enough to hold a horse's ton. What am I?

140. Break me and I get better, immediately harder to break again. What am I?

141. The sun bakes them. The hand takes them. The foot treads on them. The mouth tastes them. What are they?

142. I come in darkness and never when you call. I bring enlightenment to some, while tapping the emotions of all. What am I?

143. Some people hide me, but I will show. No matter how hard people try, never down will I go. What am I?

144. The strangest creature you'll ever find: two eyes in front and many more behind. What am I?

THIS ONE TIME . . .

A man in a movie theater notices a grasshopper sitting in the next row. He leans forward and says, "Are you a grasshopper?" The grasshopper turns and looks at him and says, "Yes." The man responds, "What are you doing at the movies?" The grasshopper replies, "Well, I like the book!"

A penguin walks into a store, goes to the counter, and says to the cashier, "Have you seen my brother?" The cashier says, "I don't know. What does he look like?"

My teachers told me I'd never amount to much because I procrastinate. I told them, "Just you wait!"

Vincent listens intently when his chemistry teacher looks at the periodic table and says, "Oxygen is a must for breathing and life. It was discovered in 1773." Vincent shakes his head and calls out, "Well, it's a good thing I was born after 1773!"

"Jane," the teacher asked, "What is the formula for water?" Jane thought for a minute and replied, *"H, I, J, K, L, M, N, O."* "No, Jane, that's supposed to be H-2-O." Jane shook her head. "That's what I said!"

Two cupcakes are in the oven baking together when one of them says, "Gee, if we don't get out of here alive, I just want to say, I love you." The other cupcake says, "Oh my gosh . . . A talking cupcake!"

A man runs into a hospital emergency room screaming, "Help me! I'm shrinking!" A nurse grabs him and sits the man down in the waiting room. "We're very busy here today, sir, you're going to have to be a little patient."

A young boy knocks on a door on Halloween night and says, "Trick or treat?" A woman opens the door, looks at him, and says, "I don't know if I can give you a treat. What are you supposed to be?" The boy pauses and answers, "A werewolf." The woman shakes her head. "But you're not wearing a costume!" With a laugh, the boy replies, "Well, it's not a full moon yet, is it?"

Shannon just got her license and drove to school. She walked in to class well after the late bell rang. The teacher looked up at her and demanded, "Why are you so late?" Shannon explained, "Because of the traffic sign." The teacher shook her head and asked, "What traffic sign?" Shannon pointed outside. "Look. The sign that says, 'School Ahead Drive Slow.'"

Cameron was planting flower seeds on a hot day, sweating from the bright sun. He wiped his brow and said, "I'm so hot." His neighbor said, "You need to wait until the sun goes down, or plant in the morning when it is coolest." Cameron said, "I can't do that. It says on the package, 'Plant in full sun!'"

A lifeguard stormed up to Aiden's mother angrily. "Tell Aiden to stop peeing in the pool!" he demanded. The mother shrugged indifferently. "Everyone knows that from time to time, young children will urinate in the pool," the mother lectured him. "Oh really?" the angry lifeguard sneered. "From the diving board?!"

Simon handed his mom a beautifully wrapped box with a birthday surprise in it. She opened it up and said, "Oh, Simon, what a pretty teapot." Simon asked eagerly, "Do you like it?" "It's lovely," she replied. "But I have a rather nice one already." Simon gulped. "Umm . . . No, you don't."

Malcolm and his mother were at the supermarket and had a long discussion about where milk comes from. The whole ride home, Malcolm was quiet. "Is everything okay, Malcolm?" his mother asked. "Yes. I'm just thinking," he replied. "What are you thinking about?" she asked. "Mama, how do cows sit on all of those little bottles?"

A father frantically called the doctor. "Doctor, doctor, my son grabbed my pen and swallowed it. What do I do?" The doctor took a deep breath and replied, "Use another one until I get there."

Frizzik the cannibal was late for dinner again. His wife, Annabul, was really angry. This was the third time in a week! Annabul's mother sat at the table chewing on a bone. The old lady grumbled, "Just give him the cold shoulder when he gets here."

A guy is walking through the woods one day when he comes across a suitcase. He takes a look inside, only to find a fox and her cubs. He calls the animal authorities and tells the woman who answers the phone what he's found. She says, "Oh, that's horrible. Are they moving?" The guy replies, "I don't know, but that would explain the suitcase."

There are special schools popping up everywhere. If you're a surfer, maybe you'll go to Boarding School. Giants have a preference for High School. King Arthur went to Knight School. The ice-cream man got his degree from Sundae School.

An elephant drinking from a stream sees a tortoise lounging on the shore. He grabs it with his trunk and flings it into the jungle. A passing zebra asked, "Why'd you do that?" The elephant said, "Forty years ago that very tortoise bit my tail just for fun." Shocked, the zebra exclaimed, "Wow, forty years ago! How'd you remember that?" To which the elephant replied, "Well, I have turtle recall."

Two cows are standing in a field eating grass. The first cow turns to the second and says, "Moooooo!" The second cow replies, "Hey, I was just about to say the same thing!"

Carl asks his mom if he can have some animal crackers. His mom gives him a box of crackers and tells him he can just have a few. His mom leaves and comes back in a few minutes, finding all the crackers on the floor with Carl looking through them. His mother asks, "What are you doing, Carl?" Carl replies, "It said, 'Don't eat if the seal is already broken.' But I can't find a seal!"

A man walks into a seafood store carrying a salmon
under his arm. "Hey, do you make fish cakes?"
he asks. "Yes, we do," replies the fishmonger.
"Great," says the man. "It's his birthday."

A man walks into a shop and sees a cute little dog. He asks the shopkeeper, "Does your dog bite?" The shopkeeper says, "No, my dog doesn't bite." The man reaches down to pet the dog and the dog bites him. "Ouch!" the man says. "I thought you said your dog doesn't bite!" The shopkeeper replies, "That's not my dog!"

Mr. and Mrs. Jones have two children. One is named Mind Your Own Business and the other is named Trouble. On the first day of school, the two kids decided to play hide-and-seek while at recess. Trouble hid while Mind Your Own Business counted to one hundred. Mind Your Own Business began looking for her brother behind hidden corners, the slide, and bushes. The bell rang ending recess and neither child got in line to reenter the school. Mind Your Own Business kept looking despite the lunch aide calling for her to get on the line. The aide approached her and asked, "What are you doing?" "Playing a game," the girl replied. "What is your name?" the aide questioned. "Mind Your Own Business." Furious, the aide inquired, "Are you looking for trouble?!" The girl looked up and replied, "Yes!"

A fly feels a bug on its back and asks, "Hey, bug on my back, are you a mite?" "I mite be," giggles the mite. "That's the worst pun I've ever heard," the fly groans. "What do you expect?" asks the mite. "I came up with it on the fly."

Grandma was babysitting little Eric. She had a stack of coins on the table and when she came into the room, they were missing. "Eric! Where are the coins?" Eric pointed to his mouth and said, "Yum." Grandma called her daughter and rushed her grandson to the hospital. Eric's parents met her there and took Eric into the emergency room. Grandma sat in the waiting room, watching the clock. An hour passed, then two. She was nervous. Grandma knocked on the glass window. "I just want to know how my grandson is doing." The attendant said she'd get the nurse. A minute later the nurse appeared. "How's Eric?" The nurse shook her head. "No change yet."

One day a fly is buzzing around a wolfhound and decides to ask him, "What kind of dog are you?" The dog replies, "I'm a wolfhound." The fly says, "A wolfhound? That's an odd name. Why do they call you that?" The dog says, "Well, it's quite simple, really. My mother was a hound, and my dad was a wolf." The fly replies, "Oh, I see . . ." Then the dog asks the fly, "So, what kind of fly are you?" The fly says, "I'm a horsefly." To which the dog says, "NOOO WAAAAYYYYY!!!"

A woman owned a rabbit farm and was known around the world for her rabbits who could lift more than any man. Wanting to start her own rabbit farm, Hallie decided she must see these rabbits. She took the train to see them. It was a long trip, but she knew if she wanted to pursue her dream of a rabbit farm, she'd have to see this one. The farmer met Hallie at the station and took her in her truck to see the farm. Sure enough, there were hundreds of rabbits. They were moving boulders with their noses. Some stood on their hind legs and were pushing wheelbarrows filled with produce. "I've never seen anything like this!" Hallie exclaimed. "Look at these rabbits; they are the strongest I've ever seen!" The farmer beamed with pride. Hallie turned to her. "You must tell me your secret. You must!" she implored. "Well," the farmer said. "It's really no secret." She reached into the pocket of her overalls and pulled out a bottle of shampoo. She pointed to the label, where in big letters it stated, "Keeps your hare strong."

Omar broke both his arms in an accident. He wore a cast on each of them from wrist to elbow. They were propped up by a big bar that held them aloft. He took a walk and paused outside a music shop. In the window was the most beautiful guitar he had ever seen. He stared at it for a long time, shook his head, and walked in the door. "How much is that guitar?" He nodded toward the instrument. "That one?" the store owner said. "It's very expensive." Omar responded, "That's all right. I'd like to buy it." The owner looked at the guitar and then back to the two casts holding up Omar's arms. "And how, may I ask, do you intend to play it?" Omar smiled. "I'll just play it by ear."

Mrs. Jackson is announcing her class's next speaker for career day, who happens to be a butcher. She says, "He has chicken wings, pig cheeks, and chicken thighs." Shocked, one of the students says, "He must be really funny looking."

A businessperson was driving down a country road when he spotted a little boy with a lemonade stand. It was hot and he was thirsty, so he decided to stop. Once he got up to the little boy's stand, he noticed a sign that said, "All-you-can-drink 10 cents," and a single, very small glass. Well, he thought that it was an awfully small glass, but since it was only a dime for all-you-can-drink, he decided to get some anyway. He gave the boy a dime and gulped down the lemonade in one swig. He slapped the glass back onto the table and said, "Fill 'er up." The kid replied, "Sure thing, that'll be 10 cents more." The businessperson said, "But your sign says, 'All-you-can-drink 10 cents.'" The little boy replied, "That's right. That's all you can drink for 10 cents."

This dog walks into a telegraph office and picks up a blank form. He writes on it, "Woof. Woof. Woof. Woof. Woof. Woof. Woof. Woof. Woof." Then he hands the form to the clerk. The clerk looks it over and says, "You know, there are only nine words here. You could add another 'Woof' for the same price." The dog shakes his head at the clerk in disbelief and says, "But then it would make no sense at all."

Two friends are walking their dogs, a Boxer and a Chihuahua, when they smell a delicious aroma coming from a nearby restaurant. The guy with the Boxer says, "Let's get something to eat." The guy with the Chihuahua replies, "We can't go in there, we have dogs with us. They are not allowed." The first guy says, "Just follow my lead." He puts on a pair of sunglasses and walks into the restaurant. "Sorry," the owner says, stopping him. "No pets allowed." "This is my Seeing Eye dog," the guy with the Boxer says. "A Boxer?" the owner asks. "Yes, they're using them now." The owner says, "Very well, then, come on in." The guy with the Chihuahua repeats the process and gets the same response from the owner: "Sorry, no pets allowed." "But this is my Seeing Eye dog," says the second guy. "A Chihuahua?" asks the owner. "A Chihuahua?!" says the man in the dark glasses. "They gave me a Chihuahua?!"

Tim points to a dog walking past him on the street.
"Do you see that dog?" he says to his friend Ralphie.
"Yeah, what about him?" Ralphie asks. Tim responds,
"He went to the flea circus and stole the show!"

Mrs. Beaks decided to teach a lesson on logical thinking. "This is the scene," said the teacher.

"A man is standing up in a boat in the middle of a river, fishing. He loses his balance, falls in, and begins splashing and yelling for help. His wife hears him, knows he can't swim, and runs down to the bank. Why do you think she ran to the bank?" One girl raises her hand proudly and asks, "To withdraw his savings?"

Two brothers, Charley and Ron, are trying to start a farm. Charley finds a prized bull in the ads and leaves to check it out. He tells Ron that he will contact him to come haul the bull back to the farm if he buys it. Charley goes to the farm and loves the bull. He decides to buy it. The farmer tells him that the bull will cost exactly $599, no less. So, Charley buys the bull and heads to town to contact Ron. The only person he can find to help him is a telegraph operator. The operator tells him, "It costs 99 cents per word. What would you like to send?" Charley replies, "Well I only have $1.00 left." He thinks for a while and tells the operator he wants to send the word "comfortable." The operator asks, "How will he know you bought the bull and want him to bring the truck from the word 'comfortable'?" Charley states, "He's a slow reader."

A man believes he is a mouse and finally goes to a doctor to get help. After some weeks of counseling, he is finally healed and has learned that he isn't a mouse after all. As the man walks out of the doctor's office, he sees a cat on the street and runs back in the office screaming, "I'm scared! There's a cat on the street!" The doctor replies, "I thought you understood now that you are not a mouse." To which the man answers, "Yes, but does the cat know that?"

An antiques dealer is walking through town and sees a cat drinking milk from a saucer in a shop window. He does a double take. The saucer is very rare. He is shocked when he realizes that the saucer is an expensive find. He must have it. He enters the shop and asks the owner, "Hey, I really like that cat. Would you be willing to sell it to me?" The store owner replies, "Not for sale." The antiques dealer, thinking quickly, responds, "I'll give you $200 for it!" The shop owner agrees, and the antiques dealer grabs the cat. He acts like he is about to leave, but then adds, "Oh, would you mind throwing in the saucer? The cat seems to like it." The shop owner replies, "No way! That's my lucky saucer. I've sold hundreds of cats since I got it."

This guy gets a parrot, but it's got a grumpy attitude. The owner tries everything to change the bird's attitude, but nothing works. Finally, in a moment of desperation, he puts the parrot in the freezer. For a few moments he hears the bird squawking, and then, suddenly, all is quiet. He opens the freezer door. The parrot steps out and says, "I'm sorry that I offended you with my actions. I ask for your forgiveness." The guy is shocked by the bird's change in attitude and is about to ask what caused the transformation when the parrot continues, "By the way, may I ask, what did the chicken do?"

Two boys, Michael and Rob, walk into a candy store. While in the store, Michael steals five candy bars and puts them in his pocket. When the boys leave, Michael brags, "I stole five candy bars, beat that!" Rob says, "No problem, just follow me." They go back into the store and Rob goes up to one of the shopkeepers. He asks the shopkeeper, "Would you like to see some magic, sir?" The man says yes, and Rob immediately opens five candy bars and eats them as fast as he can. The shopkeeper, who is now angry, demands, "Where is the magic?" Rob replies, "Ta-da! The candy bars are now in my friend's pockets."

A guy was driving past a farm one day when he noticed a beautiful horse standing in one of the fields. Hoping to buy the horse, the guy stopped and offered the farmer $500 for it. The farmer said, "Sorry, he's not for sale. He doesn't look too good." The guy said, "He looks just fine. Tell you what, I'll give you $1,000 for him." The farmer again said, "Sorry, he's not for sale. He doesn't look too good." The guy now really wanted the horse and so increased his offer to $1,500. The farmer said, "Well, he doesn't look so good, but if you want him that much, he's yours." So, the guy bought the horse and took him home. The next day he returned to the farm, furious with the farmer. The man jumped out of his car to shout at the farmer calmly raking the hay, "Hey, you cheated me! You sold me a blind horse!" The farmer looked up and responded, "I told you he didn't look too good."

A grocer puts up a sign above his turkeys, "$5 each or $20 for three." All day long, people approach him, outraged by his incorrect math, and say, "It should be $15 for three; I'll just buy three turkeys separately then." After one of his employees watches this go on all day, he asks him, "Are you going to fix the sign or what?" The grocer laughs, "Why should I stop a good thing? Before I put up the sign nobody ever bought three turkeys."

A panda walks into a diner and the diner owner decides to let him stay. The panda eats his dinner and then asks for the check. He looks at the check, nods, shoots the waiter in the knee, and leaves the restaurant. The boss runs over and looks at the table. The panda left behind an open dictionary, turned to the page with the word "panda" on it. The boss reads the description: "Panda; n. Large mammal. Eats shoots and leaves."

A young girl peeks over the counter and politely says to the sales representative, "I'm interested in buying a rabbit." The saleswoman gushes, "Oh sure, sweetie. Do you have any specific color in mind? We've got some adorable white bunnies down this aisle." The girl waves her hand. "I really don't think my boa constrictor will care what color it is!"

Lloyd goes into a pet shop and tells the owner that he needs a pet for his mother. He says that his mom lives alone and could really use some company. The pet shop owner says, "I have just what she needs: a parrot that can speak five languages. She'll be very entertained by that bird." Lloyd says he'll take the parrot and makes arrangements to have the bird delivered to his mom. A few days pass and Lloyd calls his mother. "Well, Mom, how did you like that bird I sent?" She says, "Oh, Son, he was delicious!" Shocked, Lloyd says, "Mom, you ate that bird? He could speak five languages!" His mom responds, "Well, he should have said something!"

A man has always had the dream of being in a circus. He approaches the manager of the circus and tells him, "I can do the best bird impression you have ever seen." The manager says, "That's nothing special, a lot of people can do bird impressions." The man turns and says, "Okay." Then he starts to flap his arms and flies away.

An old man went to the doctor complaining of a terrible pain in his leg. "I am afraid it's just old age," the doctor replied. "There is nothing we can do about it." The old man fumed, "That can't be! You don't know what you are doing." The doctor countered, "How can you possibly know that I am wrong?" The old man replied, "Well, it's quite obvious. My other leg is fine and it's the exact same age!"

Martin received his brand-new driver's license. The family gathered on the driveway, climbed in the car, and asked where he was going to take them for a ride for the first time. The dad immediately headed for the back seat, directly behind the new driver. "I'll bet you're back there to get a change of scenery after all those months in the front passenger seat, teaching me how to drive," says the beaming boy to his father. "Nope," his dad replied. "I'm gonna sit here and kick the back of your seat as you drive, just like you've been doing to me all these years."

Three men are traveling through the desert. They are very thirsty. They come to a mysterious waterslide in the middle of the desert that has these words written at the top: "Slide down and yell the drink of your choice. At the bottom you will find a pool of that beverage." The three men are very excited. The first man slides down and yells, "Water!" and falls into a pool of water. The next man goes down and yells, "Lemonade!" and falls into a pool full of refreshing lemonade. The final man goes down and, overwhelmed with excitement, yells, "Weeee!"

A couple walks into a hole-in-the-wall restaurant. As they're about to sit down, they notice crumbs on the seat, so they wipe down the booth and table. A waitress comes over asking what they want. "I'll take a coffee," the man says. "Me too," the woman replies, "and make sure the cup is clean." The waitress returns with their drinks and places down their cups. "Now, which one of you wanted the clean cup?"

Clyde strode into John's stable looking to buy a horse. "Listen here," said John. "I've got just the horse you're looking for. The only thing is, he was trained by a strange fellow. He doesn't stop and go in the usual way. When you need to stop you must scream 'Hey-hey.' The way to get him to move is to say 'Thank Goodness.'" Clyde nodded and thought that was easy enough. "Well, I need a horse. Fine with me. Can I take him for a test run?" he asked. John nodded. He reminded him about the weird commands and slapped the back of the horse, sending Clyde down the road. Clyde was having the time of his life. This horse could run! Clyde was galloping down the dirt road when he suddenly saw a cliff up ahead. "Stop!" he screamed, but the horse kept on going. He pulled at the reins, but the horse didn't even slow down. Not one bit. No matter how much he tried, he could not remember the words to get it to stop. "Yo-yo!" he shouted. Still, the horse just kept on speeding straight to the end of the road. He was going to fall down the steep cliff! Clyde and the horse were five feet from the cliff when Clyde suddenly remembered the right command. "Hey-hey!" he shouted as loud as he could. The horse skidded to a halt just inches from the edge of the cliff. Clyde could not believe his good luck. He looked up to the sky, breathed a deep sigh of relief, and said, "Thank Goodness."

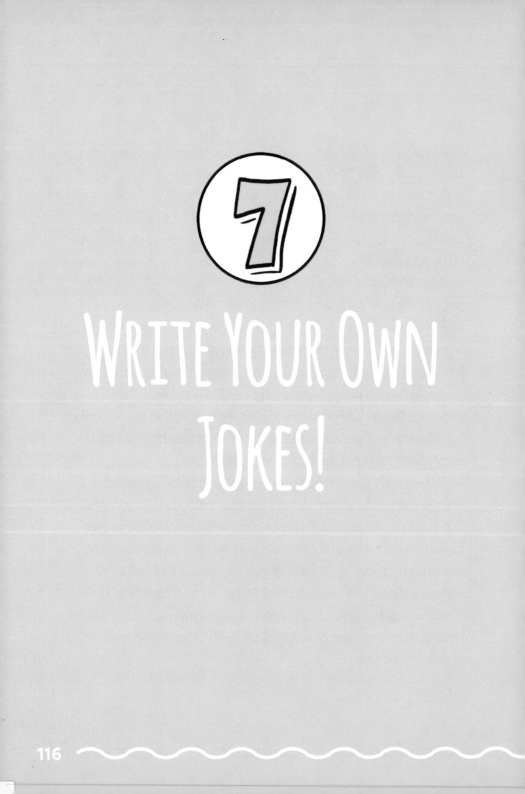

WRITE YOUR OWN JOKES!

Congratulations, Jokester! You've read hundreds of jokes and tested your comedy skills. Whether you've mastered the one-liners, told knock-knock jokes, or had tons of fun with tons of puns, you are now ready to create your own jokes.

With a few easy prompts, you'll be creating your own book of jokes in no time. Remember to keep it clean and never be hurtful or mean. Jokes are meant to make people feel good. Cheers to all of your future jokes!

I MUSTACHE YOU A QUESTION

Welcome to the first part of your joke master class. Let's start with some good, old-fashioned Q&A jokes. How do they work? Begin with a question that sets up the place or situation, for example, "Where do polar bears keep their money?" This question is a bit silly because we know polar bears don't use money. Questions can be goofy, get us thinking, or a little bit of both.

After the question comes the answer. The answer is also known as the "punch line." The punch line is a plot twist with a solution that the audience is not expecting. The answer to this joke is "a snowbank." This is a play on the word "bank," which has two meanings. Banks are buildings that keep people's money. Banks are also the edges of rivers or piles of snow. The answer "snowbank" combines both ideas, making us draw a funny picture in our heads. Here's another one: "What has hundreds of ears but can't hear a thing?"

This question will have your listener thinking of creatures with hundreds of ears. They won't be prepared for the utterly simple answer: "a cornfield."

Write a few answers for each joke question that seem funny to you. Then test them out on an audience! You will learn what works and what does not work very quickly.

Why is Cinderella no good at soccer?

A. ....

B. ....

C. ....

Hint: Think of a word that Cinderella and soccer might have in common. Cinderella goes to a ball, and soccer is played with a ball. See if you can give an answer that involves this shared word. You should also feel free to develop you own clever ideas!

Why can't you tell a joke while you're standing on ice?

A. ....

B. ....

C. ....

Hint: What do joke telling and ice have in common? They both involve "cracking." Can you create a punch line using that idea?

Why did the dinosaur cross the road?

A. ···

B. ···

C. ···

> **Hint:** *Everybody knows the old joke about the chicken. By substituting a dinosaur for the chicken, you will leave your audience puzzled, waiting for a funny response. Why would a dinosaur cross the road? (Maybe it's because chickens don't exist yet!)*

Now, let's come up with some completely original jokes. The trick is to think of simple things, then find funny twists. Look around your house and consider everyday objects. Even pets provide great joke material. Do you have a cat? Picture it sitting by a computer, then find something funny about it!

Why was the cat sitting by the computer?

A. ···

Think of a good (and funny) reason why a cat might sit by the computer. Maybe it's "To keep an eye on the mouse!"

Now you see a math book. Let's use that! We know that math books don't have emotions, but by giving the book a personality, you can create a funny joke.

Why was the math book sad?

Can you think of a reason the math book might be sad? What kinds of thing would you find in a math book? Lots of problems! That's a good reason for a math book to be sad. For what other reasons might a math book be sad?

A. ....

B. ....

C. ....

WHO'S KNOCK-KNOCKIN'?

Knock-knock jokes can be a play on words or just plain silly. Can you think of something that might work? Here's one setup: Say a name or word and think about a funny phrase to finish the punch line.

It helps to find a word that sounds like it can be used as a substitute or a rhyme for another word. Let's say you pick "Justin." Can you use the name "Justin" in a sentence? Say the name a few times and see if you can make a full sentence with it. How about "Justin time"? Now, try it in a knock-knock joke:

Knock, knock.
Who's there?
Justin.
Justin who?
Justin time to open the door for me!

Joke Factory

What might be a funny way to fill in the punch line?

Knock, knock.
Who's there?
Gladys.
Gladys who?
Gladys _____.

Hint: Doesn't the name "Gladys" sound a lot like "glad it's"? Say it fast and find a word to complete the sentence.

Knock, knock.
Who's there?
Candace.
Candace who?
Candace _____.

Hint: Try to make a sentence using the name "Candace." What would happen if we add something about opening the door? "Candace be...?"

Knock, knock.
Who's there?
Troy.
Troy who?
Troy _____.

Hint: Make a sentence with the word "Troy." With the right word combinations, it can sound a bit like "try." Troy to remember that!

Are you getting the hang of it? Now, try to fill in some knock-knock jokes with your own words and names.

Knock, knock.
Who's there?

_____.

_____who?

_____.

Knock, knock.
Who's there?

_____.

_____who?

_____.

Knock, knock.
Who's there?

_____.

_____who?

_____.

Knock, knock.
Who's there?

_____.

_____who?

_____.

Knock, knock.
Who's there?

_____.

_____who?

_____.

Time to Tongue Twist

Writing a tongue twister is a lot like writing a poem.

1. Pick a letter, any letter.
2. Write down as many words as you can think of that start with or include that sound. The more alike all your words sound, the better.
3. Make up a sentence that uses as many of your words as possible.

Let's make a list of words that each start with the letter "S." "She," "sells," "shells," and "silly" are good matches. However, "storm," "study," and "supply" are not. Can you guess why? If you said that the second set of words don't sound as similar to each other, you'd be right. Now, let's see if you can string together the words that sound alike. Which do you think makes a more fun tongue twister?

She sells silly shells.

So, study supply storm.

This time let's try with the letter "R." Now, see if you can find four words that have the same sort of sound, maybe "row," "roar," "roses," and "rice." Together, they roll off the tongue!

Row rice, roses roar.

Joke Factory

Now, let's do the same thing, with a twist!

1. Pick a sound, any sound.
2. Write down as many words as you can think of that start with or include that sound. The more alike all your words sound, the better.
3. Make up a sentence that uses as many of your words as possible.

Let's choose the sound "oo."
Choose, moose, snooze, loose

Now, string them in a sentence.
The loose moose chooses to snooze.

Can you think of another way to string these words together?

- -

Now, let's try it with the sound "in."
Tin, win, chin

Now, string them in a sentence.
A tin chin did win.

Can you think of another way to string these words together?

- -

Here are a few words that have the sound "*iss*" in them.

This   Hiss   Miss

Can you think of one more?

. . . .

Now, let's make a sentence with them:

. . . .

How many other letters and sounds can you make tongue twisters with?

Letter . . . .

Twist! . . . .

Letter . . . .

Twist! . . . .

Sound . . . .

Twist! . . . .

Sound . . . .

Twist! . . . .

Something punny is going on...

Some puns are created by using similar-sounding words, such as "slice" and "nice." The joke might look like this:

**What does a pizza say
when it introduces itself to you?**
"Slice to meet you."

Others are a play on a word or part of a word with two meanings, like the "tiles" part of "reptiles."

How did dinosaurs decorate their bathrooms?
With reptiles.

Joke Factory

Now, let's play with puns in a sentence. What word best works here?

**Two silkworms got into a race
and ended in a _____.**

If you said "tie," that would be perfect! Why? Because these silkworms are racing, so they could end in a *tie*. Silkworms also create beautiful silk from their cocoons that can be used to make a *tie*—the kind you wear. It's clever because the same word (spelled the same, too!) has two meanings.

How do you fix a broken tomato?

If you said "tomato paste," that's a great answer! Tomato paste is something you put in pasta. And we all know that paste (like glue) is something we use to put things back together, or fix them. This joke plays with the double meaning of the word "paste."

Can you think of any more plays on words? Try brainstorming a few words that have double meanings, such as "buy" and "by" and "ate" and "eight."

Now, can you use the words you came up with to make some punny jokes?

Now let's make up some puns using the following cartoons. Let your imagination expand as the picture guides you. Remember: There are no wrong answers!

Hint: *What might you say if it's a little cold out?*

Hint: *What might you say to a friend who is super funny?*

Riddle Me This

You can think of riddles as the brainteasers of jokes. The idea is to stump your audience, but not too much! You want them to have to use their noggins just a bit in order to solve your clever riddle. Here's how to start making a riddle:

1. Begin with the answer.

2. Think of the things your answer does and what it looks like.

3. Then create a question or situation that leads you to your answer. That's your riddle!

> ### A few tips:
>
> • Try imagining objects reacting as if they are human. Think about what they are doing or saying.
>
> • Use simple words.

Here's an example to get you thinking.

I put my head in the ground and my feet in the air. What am I?

I bet you were thinking about how a person could possibly do that! Puns make you think outside the box. When we give human characteristics to a vegetable, the whole picture comes into focus. What vegetable has its head buried in the ground while its body is up in the air? How about an onion?

The head or bulb is buried in the ground while its stems or legs are high above in the air! In this example, if we start with the idea of an onion and think about how its head is buried in the ground, then we can work backward and develop a joke around it. What other riddles can you create? Be patient with yourself, as riddles can be challenging. The important part is to make notes as ideas come to you (that's what pro comedians do!). And most important, keep trying!

Master of Jokes

As we've learned, the setup is the first part of a joke that sets up the laugh. Its whole job is to create expectations and grab the audience's attention. The punch line is the second part. The punch line makes you laugh because it reveals the surprise. Let's take this longer joke apart to see how it's done when we have more than one or two lines:

One day, Max went to see Carl. Carl had a big, swollen nose. *(We're setting up the story.)*

"Whoa, what happened, Carl?" Max asked. *(The listeners are now engaged. They want to know why Carl has a swollen nose. This is what they are expecting to hear.)*

"I sniffed a brose," Carl replied. *(Now the listener is surprised.)*

"What?" Max said. "There's no 'b' in 'rose'!" *(Still drawing suspense before the punch line . . .)*

Carl replied, "There was in this one!" *(The punch line—aka the surprise!—is that the letter "b" turned out to be a **bee!**)*

Five Rules of Joke Writing

If you want to tell jokes, you have to see the humor in everyday life. Here are five easy steps:

1. Change your perspective. Look at things from different angles and find the quirky relationships they may have to other things. Just think of all the plays on words we had above.

Why is Cinderella no good at soccer?
Because she is always running away from the ball!

2. Be quick! Look around you and find things that may have multiple meanings, like when you are in an ice-cream store and you see them scooping ice-cream.

What was the reporter doing at the ice-cream shop?
Getting the scoop!

3. Look beyond the surface of things. On the surface a rock may just be a rock, but look a little deeper and you may have a rock band.

What rock group has four guys who don't sing?
Mount Rushmore.

4. See the funnier side of life. A clown-eating lion would be far from funny, but just picture the unsatisfied lion spitting out a clown.

Why did the lion spit out the clown?
Because he tasted funny!

5. Have fun! Life is better when we fill it with laughs.

A skunk fell in the river and stank to the bottom.
Of course he did!

Joke Factory

See if you can put all of your joke-telling skills and joke-writing knowledge into making up your very own longer jokes. Take time to think about your setups and punch lines. It might surprise you what goes together to deliver the final laugh!

Setup:

. . . .

. . . .

. . . .

Punch Line!

. . . .

. . . .

. . . .

Remember: Joke telling and joke writing are not about being perfect. They're about trying, learning, and getting better each time. Even the best comedians bomb on their way to making us crack up!

Riddle Answers

1. An elephant's shadow!
2. A hole.
3. A telephone.
4. Short.
5. He's alive.
6. A goose.
7. A rhinoceros.
8. An automobile.
9. A tennis ball.
10. A coat of paint.
11. A flag.
12. A relationship.
13. Neither, they both burn shorter!
14. A scale.
15. A stamp.
16. Because all his uncles are ants.
17. A horse.
18. Wrong.
19. Eight. Horses have hooves and chickens have claws. Only the four humans, the farmer and his family, have feet.
20. He is walking.
21. The president.
22. Your voice.
23. Stars.
24. It wasn't raining.
25. Because the batteries died.
26. A shadow.
27. "O I C U R M T."
28. The letter "m."
29. Pilgrims.
30. Gold.
31. Just fine. People have fingers on both hands!
32. She was born on February 29, in a leap year!
33. A deck of cards.
34. A battery.
35. The match.
36. Plates.
37. A reflection.
38. A feather.
39. A cowboy riding his horse.

40. Because it has four eyes but it cannot see!

41. An umbrella.

42. "Alphabet."

43. Legs.

44. The word "ton."

45. The letter "g."

46. Footsteps.

47. The one with the biggest head.

48. None. He has three sisters.

49. Three.

50. She fell from the bottom step.

51. A street.

52. A catcher and an umpire.

53. "Underground."

54. Money.

55. Age.

56. A pillow.

57. Rain.

Bonus Math Riddle 1:
$888 + 88 + 8 + 8 + 8 = 1000$.

58. The letter "D."

59. The alphabet.

60. Misspelled!

61. A deal.

62. A shadow.

63. Three: one blonde, one brunette, and one redhead.

64. An address.

65. "NOON."

66. A tree.

67. A brain.

68. A mirror.

69. A straw-berry.

70. A tree.

71. "Few."

72. Thunder.

73. "Queue."

74. A mirror.

75. Charcoal.

76. A key.

77. When it's frozen.

78. The letter "k."

79. A promise.

80. A book.

81. "Empty."

82. A shoe.

83. A cabbage.

84. Your word.

85. The moon.

86. A lightbulb.

87. A pillow.

88. Ohio.

89. Your finger.

90. Edam.

91. C-A-T.

92. A refrigerator.

93. A flight of stairs.

94. The sun.

95. A football match.

96. A brook.

97. A mirror.

98. A match.

99. A deck of cards.

100. A shirt.

101. The letter "L."

102. A stapler.

103. Sawdust.

104. A pen.

105. Day and night.

106. A dictionary.

107. A compass.

108. A snowman.

109. Eyes.

110. A nest.

111. A snake.

Bonus Math Riddle 2: The answer has to do with time! If 11:00 a.m. plus two hours is 1:00 p.m., then 9:00 p.m. plus five hours is 2:00 a.m.

112. A fish.

113. It churned the cream to make butter!

114. The chain was not attached to anything!

115. A bowling ball knocked down 10 pins!

116. A book!

117. A coin.

118. A feather.

119. Nothing.

120. The ocean.

121. A cherry.

122. She is reading braille.

123. An icicle.

124. They only sleep at night.

125. Zero seconds. The house was already built by the first 20 people!

126. A broom.

127. Corn.

128. Eat. (ate)

129. Cubes only have six sides.

130. Neither, the yolks of eggs are yellow.

131. No, because he is already dead.

132. A queen bee.

133. Lightning

134. A lizard.

135. When you're a mouse.

136. Ten. (We can call the pigs cows, but that doesn't make them cows.)

137. Ice.

138. Imagination.

139. Human hair.

140. A world record.

141. Grapes.

142. A dream.

143. Age.

144. A peacock.

Build Your Own Comedy Library

365 Jokes for Kids: A Joke A Day Book by Chrissy Voeg

The Big Book of Silly Jokes for Kids: 800+ Jokes! by Carole P. Roman

Knock, Knock! Who's There? My First Book of Knock-Knock Jokes by Tad Hills

Silly Jokes for Silly Kids by Silly Willy

A Whole Lotta Knock-Knock Jokes: Squeaky-Clean Family Fun by Mike Spohr and Heather Spohr

About the Author

CAROLE P. ROMAN is the award-winning author of more than 50 children's books. Whether they are about pirates, princesses, or discovering the world, her books have enchanted educators, parents, and children. She hosts the podcast *Indie Authors Roundtable* and is one of the founders of the magazine *Indie Authors Monthly*. She is the author of the bestselling *The Big Book of Silly Jokes for Kids: 800+ Jokes!* and *Spies, Code Breakers, and Secret Agents: A World War II Book for Kids*. In addition to joke books and adventure stories, she published *Mindfulness for Kids: 30 Activities to Stay Calm, Happy & In Control* with J. Robin Albertson-Wren. *The Big Book of Silly Jokes 2* is her second joke book. Carole lives on Long Island, where she likes to read and crack jokes with her children and grandchildren.

About the Illustrator

DYLAN GOLDBERGER is an illustrator and printmaker based in Brooklyn, New York. He grew up in New Rochelle and moved to Brooklyn in 2007 to attend Pratt Institute, graduating with a BFA in communication design. His self-published alphabet book, *See Spot Shred*, released in 2015, shows his love of dogs and skateboarding, recurring themes throughout his artwork. When he's not working in the studio, he's out exploring the parks and streets of New York City with his dog Townes. His illustrations have been used by many notable brands and publications.